GREEN HAND

The life of a fisherman is a hard one. 'Mondays to Fridays he takes his boat to sea, Saturdays he takes his thirst to a pub, and Sundays he takes his wife to bed. And by God, by the time Monday morning's come around his wife is that sick of him that she's as pleased as the seagulls to get him off to sea again.' David Jones did not take long to see the reason why.

Lillian Beckwith

Green Hand

A novel

ARROW BOOKS

ARROW BOOKS LTD
178–202 Great Portland Street, London W1

AN IMPRINT OF THE · HUTCHINSON GROUP

London Melbourne Sydney
Auckland Bombay Toronto
Johannesburg New York

❋

First published by
Hutchinson & Co (*Publishers*) Ltd 1967
Arrow edition 1969

*Made and printed in Great Britain
by The Anchor Press Ltd,
Tiptree, Essex*

09 002500 8

In memory of the 'Bosun'

Chapter 1

He'd arrived too late in the day to have any luck. The suspicion along with its accompanying depression had begun to assert itself more than an hour before the train, with himself the solitary passenger in the whole of one coach, had started to slide into the station. He would have liked the train to have rushed in, announcing its arrival with a great gout of fussy steam; to have found the platform thronged with people: people arriving, people greeting, people departing. But this was the railhead; the destination that of a small Scottish fishing port; and it was Saturday evening. The train rumbled along the platform until with a barely perceptible jolt the engine met the buffers. The only person visible, a lofty porter, stood with arms akimbo looking archly along the length of the train as if challenging it to produce passengers. With a shudder it produced David and also five boiler-suited, cloth-capped, wise-cracking railwaymen who spilled out from a compartment close to the engine. There had been plenty of passengers when the train had left the mainline station, mostly housewives who after a speculative glance at the empty seats of his compartment and then a dubious assessment of his scowling face and thick black beard had passed on, leaving him to stretch himself over the waste of seats. David had grinned with satisfaction. Gradually the train had emptied, leaving a trickle of women at each of the tiny country stations. Disinterestedly he had watched them mustering their innumerable parcels and baskets around them on the platform; heard them remonstrating with welcoming off-spring and shouting good-humoured farewells to the guard and engine driver. He had allowed himself to think of them going home to their suppers of goodies from the town shops but the thought of their feasting only made him more aware of his own hunger and he had forced himself to concentrate on other things.

The porter exchanged a few words of badinage with the railwaymen. The driver, alighting from his engine, added a quip of his own. A derisive shout from the guard at the rear of the train provoked a burst of equally derisive laughter and the group were still flinging nimble-tongued taunts along the length of the platform as they disappeared through the ticket office and out into the grey light beyond.

As he handed his ticket to the porter the man gave David a nod of attempted recognition.

'So you're back,' he said.

'Aye,' David agreed, appreciating the man's dilemma. He had no recollection of ever having seen the porter before and he doubted if the man recollected him but he had learned that the Highlander considers it the height of discourtesy to fail to recognise even the most cursory acquaintance. The porter was obviously taking no risks.

'Holiday?' he queried. It was the beginning of October—too late in the year for a small Scottish fishing port to be much of an attraction for visitors.

David grinned one-sidedly. 'You could call it that,' he said. He didn't want to tell the porter that he had started his journey in the high hope of joining the *Silver Spray* this very evening.

The man's interest quickened but the thumps of boxes being hurled on to the platform from the rear of the train sent him loping in that direction. With an assumed air of purposefulness David adjusted the straps of his rucksack and followed the path of the railwaymen. The station opened directly on to the pier so that the moment one stepped out one was confronted by the mingled smells and sights and sounds of the sea and its industry. Fish and tar and fuel oil; the swinging network of masts; trucks and trolleys abandoned for the weekend, thousands and thousands of stacked fishboxes; the yodelling and screaming of gulls, the ringing shouts of children. Except for the gulls and about half a dozen children there was little activity on the pier. The gulls, though obviously sated on the refuse of the morning's catch, still probed with muttered optimism among the debris of the pier for fish that had been pounded into oil by the wheels of heavy lorries. The children picked up dead crabs and lobsters, examined them briefly for signs of life and finding none hurled them into the sea to join the jettisoned fishboxes, newspapers and whole loaves of bread that still floated in the harbour. The rows of boats, their holds empty, jostled one another at their moorings. The offices of the fish buyers were deserted.

David leaned on the rail, inhaling deep, satisfying breaths of the sea-spiced air; letting the damp wind blow coolly through his thatch of hair; feeling it tautening the skin of his travel-weary face. His questing gaze roamed over the moored boats, seeking anxiously for the familiar white hull and green capping of Donald's launch and when he could see no sign of her he let his eyes caress the serried ranks of ringnetters with their trim decks and varnished hulls; dark painted drifters, their drabness enlivened by the brightly coloured netfloats that were piled in their sterns. There were smaller boats too that interested him: lobster boats, he surmised; and an in-between-sized boat, green-painted and with a couple of barrels on her deck and her hold covered by a new tarpaulin. A motor-yacht with so much white superstructure that she resembled a howdah on an elephant caught his eye but reject-

ing it disdainfully he turned away and walked down towards
the end of the pier to where a large old-fashioned boat, now
obviously convert d for cargo carrying, lay alongside. The
name *Spiʒannah* was painted in curly gold lettering across her
ample stern. She had apparently finished discharging, for an
oilskinned figure was engaged in sweeping down the decks.
Suddenly David was aware of an urchin crouching beside
him, a large dead crab in his hand. The urchin rose stealthily,
flung the crab with an exuberant aim and then crouched again
behind a trio of barrels. The crab hit the figure on *Spiʒannah*'s
deck slap in the back of its sou'westered head, causing it to
stumble forward and trip over the brush so that it almost fell
headlong. The figure regained its balance, turned, and with a
shrill stream of abuse picked up the crab and hurled it at
David. The crab fell short so that it hit the pier and went into
the sea. The voice, David conjectured, could have been either
that of a young boy or of a girl but the inexpertness of the aim
made him decide it was exclusively feminine. He found himself hoping it wasn't a girl. He disapproved of girls using such
language as he had just heard.

Another oilskinned figure was approaching now along the
pier—a small wizened male this time who climbed aboard the
Spiʒannah and after a brief exchange of comments the two
went below. The urchin, who had been keenly watching
events from the safety of his hide, gave David a conspiratorial
grin and ran off to join his friends.

David wandered back along the pier and leaned again on
the rail, looking out over the petulant sea to where the deep
grey outlines of the islands seemed only emphatic shadows
between the grey of sea and sky. He might have been dis-
couraged by the drabness of the scenery had he not known
that it was only one of the many moods of this bewildering
coast. Tomorrow's dawn could come like the sudden flicking
open of a shabby jewel-case to reveal the untold splendour
inside. Tomorrow that sky might be a scudding of white

4

over blue, patching the rumpled islands with moving sunlight and kindling the sea to the iridescence of a peacock's spread tail. His eye discerned an incisive bow-wave white among the grey and his spirits soared as he made out that it was a small motor-boat making her way towards the harbour. It was not coming from the direction he would have expected Donald to come in the *Silver Spray* but then Donald was as unpredictable as the sea itself. He might easily have gone out of his way to pick up a little feminine company for the weekend; or he might just have become so engrossed in a good thriller that he had not paid sufficient attention to the helm. All aspects of the unexpected could happen when Donald was alone in a boat. David stared at the approaching shape fixedly but as it drew closer he realised with growing despondency that it was not the *Silver Spray*.

Two young boys, scruffy-suited and ruddy-cheeked, came to lean on the rail beside him, examining him surreptitiously.

'Seen anything of the *Silver Spray*?' he asked them, trying to make his voice sound unconcerned.

The bigger of the two reflected a moment before answering, but the other replied instantly.

'No, I didn't see her yet.'

'No,' confirmed the bigger boy. 'I didn't see her yet, either.'

'You know the one I mean?' There was a trace of testiness in David's voice now.

'Surely. She's Donald Beag's boat. Him that has the long red hair and is always chasin' after the girls.'

David decided they knew Donald perfectly well.

'Was she in last Saturday?' he asked them.

'Indeed, I don't remember seein' her at all. Not for a week or two now.' Again it was the smaller boy who answered.

'Indeed, I don't remember seein' her myself, either,' corroborated his companion dutifully.

There were murmurings of panic along with the empty

rumblings in David's stomach. What if Donald had at last carried out his often-expressed threat to sell the boat and have done with the sea. He was foolish not to have thought of it before, he chided himself.

Satisfied that they had discovered the stranger's quest, the boys waited only a moment for further questions before darting off to impart the news to the curious.

Two more boys of a roughly similar size and age appeared pushing a truck loaded with cardboard boxes from the direction of the village and came to a halt at the top of the harbour steps. David moved his position to watch them. They gave him a swift glance of appraisal before starting to lift the first of the boxes from the truck and manœuvre it down the steps. The box looked heavy, the steps were slimy with tide-washed weed and ingrained oil but sturdy and surefooted in their sloppy gumboots the boys struggled and heaved it on to the deck of the nearest boat. Not until they had unloaded all the boxes from the truck did they pay any attention to the labels and then, shouting questions and instructions to each other, they worked together on the hazardous task of hauling the boxes from deck to swaying deck.

'Did we get the *Catriona*'s bread, Tommy?'

'No, we're to bring it down next time when we bring the stuff for the *Virgin*.'

Flinging back hatches they were lowering the boxes into the fo'c'sles of the boats when another truck arrived, this time in charge of the two boys David had already spoken to. They yelled an impudent question and immediately the outraged face of Tommy appeared above a hatchway. He yelled back vituperatively.

'Leave it alone, you slobs! It's our job this week. You took your turn last week.' He spoke down the hatchway. 'Hamish, come and look what these greedy slobs are at.'

Tommy's head gave way to Hamish's. 'Get off or I'll shag ye!' he shouted.

The two interlopers, returning the abuse with graphic competence, began to drag the first of their boxes down the steps. Hamish and Tommy came leaping across the decks to defend their rights and there, on the treacherous steps with a few fathoms of water waiting to receive them if they slipped, a scuffle began.

Christ! David thought, one of them's bound to go in sooner or later. He was wondering whether they could swim and whether he ought to interfere when there came a stentorian yell from close at hand. He looked round to see a tall figure in blue jeans and speckled fisherman's sweater striding towards the steps. The boys saw him too and ceased their scuffling. The man roared another threat and with glowering looks and a display of cautious amity the boys then combined to get the second batch of boxes distributed among the various boats.

The newcomer, dour-faced and grim-mouthed, watched them. There was a rumbling of stomach noises and David, tensing his muscles, realised that they were not from his own. The man gave a long belch and with the relief of wind the dourness of his expression relaxed. He nodded at David.

'There'll be one or more of 'em in the harbour if they don't get sworn at,' he explained.

David thought he recognised the man as an erstwhile drinking companion at the local bar when the *Silver Spray* had been in on one of her Saturday trips.

'They're tough little blighters,' he observed. 'Seem pretty keen on their job, too.'

'Ach, they get paid by the shops for delivering. That's the reason for the arguing.' He belched again. 'Not but what you would be able to keep the kids in this place away from the boats anyway. Look at those little nippers now!' With a proud grin he indicated a couple of tots who were struggling with a heavy hosepipe intent on washing down the pier as they had seen their fishermen fathers do.

'It's a wonder there isn't an accident,' David said.

'Ach, they're born to it. Been hanging round the pier since they could walk, most of them. It doesna do to worry in this place.' He pulled out a packet of cigarettes and held one out to David. 'Smoke?' he asked casually.

David took it, trying not to betray his yearning for it. 'Aren't you Noddy, the skipper of the *Fair Lassie*?' he ventured.

The man's eyes flicked with surprise. 'Aye, so I am,' he responded cordially but with dubious recognition. There was half a minute's pause as they both drew on their cigarettes.

'It's no' makin' such a bad day of it now,' Noddy said with a companionable glance at the grey clouds that were shredding themselves on the jagged hills. 'But it was pretty coarse till near six o'clock this morning. We had a fair pastin' comin' back to port.'

David could sense that while Noddy was talking he was straining to recollect where he had seen him before. He waited, a little smugly, giving him more time before offering enlightenment. At length he said:

'I was hoping to see the *Silver Spray* here. She doesn't seem to be in yet.'

'The *Silver Spray*!' Noddy exclaimed, his eyes bright with recognition. 'Ach, now, that's where I've seen you before.' He stretched out a strong and ready hand and clasped David's, exulting that he had at last identified him. 'You were with Donald in the *Spray* way back in the spring for a week or two. Isn't that it?'

'That's right,' David replied, reflecting ironically that the 'week or two' had in fact stretched to the best part of two months.

'Well, boy, you're unlucky then,' Noddy commiserated. 'Donald's away to the hospital with his stomach. His boat's not been in for these three weeks past.'

'Just my bloody luck,' David said, his stomach hollow

with a disappointment that was no doubt aggravated by the fact that his only food during the past forty-eight hours had been a single bar of chocolate. He gazed gloomily into the water of the harbour, cursing his luck and regretting his rashness of not waiting for Donald's reply to his telegram informing him that he proposed to join him.

'Were you supposed to be meetin' him here, then?' Noddy asked. 'It's funny nobody let you know.'

'It wasn't definitely fixed,' David admitted. It was less than a half truth. David himself had only become aware of his intention forty-eight hours previously.

'Ach, well. It's a shame nobody let you know.'

It was more than a shame. And he didn't know what he could do about it.

'Maybe one of the boats could drop you off at Donald's place on Monday when they go out,' suggested Noddy. 'There's sure to be one of them going that way, more than likely.' He meditated a moment. 'I daresay I could drop you off myself for the matter of that,' he offered. 'It wouldn't be till we'd finished settin' the creels but you'd get there sometime. How would that do you?'

'His wife wouldn't be expecting me,' David demurred.

'Ach, no matter. She'll be glad of your company with Donald out of the way.' He winked suggestively. 'A well-set-up young man like yourself. It'll make a nice change for her.'

David debated the suggestion only for a matter of seconds, envisaging the all-woman household now that Donald was away—Donald's wife, his shrewish mother, his mentally retarded sister and his undisciplined child. Oh, they'd make him welcome right enough: their hospitality was boundless but it was too easy a solution, too much of an anticlimax to his high-hearted plans. That was not the sort of life he'd burned his boats to achieve.

'Better not,' he said with a rueful smile.

9

'Aye, well, it was a thought anyway,' said Noddy. 'And if you change your mind you'll let me know and I'll get somebody to drop you.' He threw the butt of his cigarette into the water and took out another. 'You'll come up to the bar and have a dram, then?' he invited. 'All the boys'll be there. Maybe you'll hear somethin' of Donald himself and when he'll be comin' back likely.'

'No, thanks,' David said. 'I'm off it.' It was the only thing he could say. He had one and sixpence in his pocket and the fisherman's drink, as he well knew, was never less than a double whisky.

Noddy shot him a probing glance. 'Never!' he reprimanded.

'It's true enough,' David affirmed with an emphatic raising of his eyebrows. It was no excuse for not standing Noddy a drink though, and he sweated with embarrassment, hating to be thought tight-fisted.

'Aye, well, if you're not in so much of a hurry for a drink maybe you'd like to come and give me a hand to pump out the old *Skart*,' Noddy said. 'From the look of her she's badly wantin' it and if I don't do it the rest'll not stir themselves, I doubt.'

Together they went over to the far side of the pier and on board a neglected-looking boat which lay slackly alongside.

'She doesn't look as if she gets much use,' David observed after a brief inspection of her rough decks and flaking paintwork.

'Nor does she,' admitted Noddy as he worked the pump. 'The fellow that owns her has gone off this two years back and never taken a look at the boat since. Just left her here to rot to pieces. I've seen her with water up to her engine room sometimes when there's nobody been near her.'

'He didn't leave anyone in charge of her?' David asked incredulously.

'No, he did not then. Just left the poor old boat and went

off. Some say he's in America. Wherever he is, I doubt we'll ever see him in this port again.'

'She's been a good boat, too,' murmured David, eyeing the solidness of her timbers.

'Aye, she's a good boat yet. Too good for the bastard that had her. He was a man that had no heart in him at all and a fellow like that doesn't deserve to have a boat. You know these societies they have for prevention of cruelty? Well, I'd like to see one for the prevention of cruelty to boats.'

'You say he was a right bastard but you still pump his boat out for him. Why?' David pointed out, although he knew what the reply would be before he asked the question.

He was not prepared however for the flicker of anguish that betrayed itself on Noddy's face as he spoke: 'Aye, but it's more than a man can bear to see a boat suffer so.'

He gave a final burst of pumping and after a speculative glance that made sure nothing else was in need of urgent attention climbed back on to the pier.

David spoke. 'I suppose as there's no one in charge of her nobody would mind if I bunked aboard her for the weekend, would they?' It seemed to him to offer a better prospect of comfort than the bench in the station waiting room which appeared to be his only alternative.

Noddy stopped in his stride, complete comprehension on his face. 'Why would you want to bunk in a damp cold place like that when there's a bunk on my own boat to spare,' he offered. 'Plenty of room there.' He pointed towards the *Fair Lassie* which David saw was the green boat with the tarpaulin covering the hold.

'Thanks, I'll do that,' David responded, trying without much success to sound offhand. 'That'll do me fine.' Degrees happier, he turned to scan the jostling of shops and sheds and houses that comprised the village, their arrangement owing nothing to any planning scheme but looking rather as if they might once have been deposited by the tide and gradually become inhabited.

'Will there be a tea-place open?' he asked Noddy.

'Aye, there will be surely. But a good dram would do you better than a cup of tea, boy. Come away with me now. I owe you a drink for getting that box of lobsters for us when we nearly lost it that time. You mind that now?'

'Good Lord!' David exclaimed, recalling a certain Saturday afternoon when the *Silver Spray* had been tied up in the harbour waiting for her inebriated skipper to sleep off his excesses. Due to stormy weather in the north some of the boats had been late coming in. David had been watching these boats hurriedly unloading their catches when suddenly there had come a ringing cry from Noddy's boat where one of the crew, clumsy with haste, had let a precious box of lobsters slide over the side and into the water. The lid of the box had slid from under the rope and in a matter of seconds the live lobsters would have flicked their tails and returned to the sea. David, idly watching from the bows of the *Silver Spray*, had instantly grabbed a boat-hook and almost before the box had hit the water had its rope securely. With only one lobster having escaped the box was soon back aboard the *Fair Lassie* and David was glowing under the commendation of the crew. It was a small enough incident but Noddy it seemed had by no means forgotten it.

'Aye, just that,' he agreed. 'I promised the boys I'd give you a good dram for it next time I saw you so you'll not say no to me now?'

'I'd best get a bite to eat first,' David hedged. 'I'd sooner not drink on an empty stomach.'

'Right enough, I could do with a bite myself,' Noddy responded. 'Come on then, boy. Let's get to it before the place is shut for the night.' He indicated David's rucksack. 'You may just as well not burden yourself with that,' he advised. 'No one'll touch it if you leave it on top of that pile of boxes.'

'There's nothing worth pinching in it,' David told him, as he slid the rucksack off his shoulders. 'Only a pair of gumboots and a torch with its battery nearly flat.'

'You'll not need those where you're goin',' Noddy said, urging David to follow him.

Chapter 2

Of the pattern of exits that led away from the pier only one by virtue of its width could suitably have been called a road. It was an obedient road that had seeped as if by capillary attraction up the hillside to serve the scattered houses which a newly prospering and clamorous fishing industry had managed to wrest from an indifferent council. On to this road had been grafted half a dozen or so minor tracks which ended, some of them almost before they began, in a cul-de-sac or in the bog and heather of the moors.

The tea-shop to which Noddy escorted David offered little in the way of refinements. It was to outward appearance a sweet-and-tobacco shop but one or two plastic-topped tables and varnished wood chairs packed closely together served to justify its claim to be a 'Tea Room'. Noddy pulled a couple of chairs out to face the counter and leaned his elbow on the table.

'Two cups of tea and a good plate of cookies, Bessie, my lass,' he commanded in a jestingly stentorian tone as a woman of about fifty or so appeared behind the counter. She had a thin mouth that looked for ever on the point of remonstrance but her eyes appraised David with interest.

'Hi there!' David said with an impudent grin.

Her reply was a coy relaxing of the thin lips. She picked up a plate of cookies and shuffled across to their table. She was wearing carpet slippers; her hair was a shoulder-length grey frizz; her large breasts and heavy hips were shrouded in a green wrap-overall which, as she leaned over the table, gave off the mingled smells of milky tea and detergent.

'You're no' very busy,' commented Noddy.

'How would we be busy when the bar's open?' she retorted. Her voice was indifferent but the smile she slid at David as she set down a slopping cup of tea in front of him was by no means indifferent. David thought a wink would not be too committal and was amused to see the swift retaliatory droop of an eyelid. As she retreated to the back of the shop she turned and threw him a blatant look over her shoulder.

Noddy and David exchanged grimaces.

'Aye, she'll try it on with you, will Bessie,' confided Noddy in a murmur that was too loud for the small room.

'She's a bit long in the tooth for a tart, isn't she?' David whispered. 'She ought to be over it by now.'

'She's a widow,' explained Noddy. 'It takes them like that sometimes when they've no man. Stands to reason. Some of the men here thinks it's a sort of obligement on them when a woman's left on her own. Not serious like. Just an obligement,' he reiterated. 'Mind you, Bessie won't be here much longer, they tell me. She's supposed to be going back to the East coast next month, where she came from.' He spooned four heaped teaspoonsful of sugar into his cup, dug through the tea with a spoon and then gulped down a couple of mouthfuls. He then pulled a cookie into two pieces, rammed them into his mouth in quick succession and took a couple more gulps of tea which emptied his cup.

'How's the fishing?' David asked.

'No' bad. No' bad at all,' he replied, spitting wet crumbs across the table.

'What are you at yourself? Lobsters?' The neighbours at home had always maintained that David was a born mimic and now the jargon he had heard so much when he had been with Donald came easily to his tongue.

'Aye, aye, still the lobsters.' Noddy broke another cookie.

'They're still around? It's a bit late in the season, isn't it? I thought they were usually finished by this time.'

'No, no. They're scarce right enough but they're not away altogether. The season might last another three weeks or more, I reckon, depending on the weather.'

'Good prices?' David enquired.

'Bloody good prices just now.' Noddy chewed sketchily at his cookie. 'We were up north last week and brought in twelve boxes.'

'Pretty fair,' David said, hoping he sounded knowledgeable.

'Aye, fair enough for the time of year,' agreed Noddy. 'It's a wage.'

'How many creels have you out?' David bit into his second cookie, chewing it slowly and wondering if he was going to have enough money to pay for it.

'Two hundred round about.' Noddy picked up his cup from the saucer and took it over to the counter. 'Here, Bessie, give us another cup of tea,' he instructed and while she was filling his own he snatched David's cup from under his nose.

'Empty that away and give him some fresh,' he told her. 'Cold tea's no bloody good to anybody.'

David knew now that he could stop worrying how much the snack was going to cost him. Noddy had chosen this off-hand way to show that he had appointed himself host. Hungrily David tucked into his third cookie.

As soon as he had drunk his second cup of tea Noddy stood up, impatient to be off. He banged some silver on the counter and not asking how much or waiting for change he hurried David outside.

'Okay then. Now I have just to call in at the telephone on our way up to meet the boys.'

It was dark now as Noddy led the way to a telephone kiosk situated in the angle between two walls. David heard him hunting in his pockets for change; heard him swear and then saw him approaching with enquiry on his face. He's going to ask me for change, he though despairingly. But Noddy asked: 'I suppose you wouldn't know any good messages for a weddin'?' He creased one eye and looked at David.

'No,' David replied, puzzled until he remembered the Highlanders' exuberant habit of sending lewd telegrams whenever there was a wedding.

'One of the lads had gone off and got himself married this afternoon and I'll need to send him a wire. I've been tryin' to think of a good one but all the ones I can remember have been used up already.' He wrinkled his brow in a deep frown. 'The one I was just going to send is a bit tame but I thought maybe you'd know some good ones from where you've come from.'

David forbore telling him that in the small Welsh village he came from the sending of a lewd telegram would almost certainly have brought an official reprimand if not a summons. 'I don't know any offhand but I expect we could make one up if we got our heads together,' he offered.

'Ach, there's not time,' replied Noddy forlornly.

'I do remember Donald sending one once when I was with him,' David recalled. 'It was about a dining-room table . . .'

'Aye, havin' four legs and no drawers.' Noddy brightened for an instant. 'I mind that one but somebody's already sent it,' he ended gloomily. He shrugged his shoulders. 'Well, time's gettin' on so I'd best send somethin'.' He lifted the receiver and shouted at the operator. The message too was shouted so that though David had wandered several yards away he could hear each word distinctly: 'Tonight she'll be in your arms, tomorrow she'll be in your pockets—no, pockets! *Pockets!*' There came the noise of coins being inserted, and then the thump of the kiosk door.

'The operator can't have heard that one before anyway,' said Noddy satisfied. 'She couldn't seem to get it. I expect she thought it was too ordinary.' He sighed. 'They'll be disappointed in me when they get it. I can usually think of somethin' pretty good. Sometimes when we're quiet in the fo'c'sle and we're too tired to read we spend the time makin' up telegrams to send to the next weddin'. Eggo now, he's a great lad at them but mostly they're too bad for the minister to read out. I'll just have to give more time to them myself,' he went on. 'But ach! if a man gave the time and thought to them we used to in the old days he'd never get any sleep there's that much marryin' now.'

The lights of the pub were visible by this time. 'Come on and we'll find Brad and Eggo and tell them you're sleepin' aboard.'

David's tongue was hanging out for a drink and the prospect of the warmth and companionship of the bar was exceedingly attractive, but all the same he hesitated before following Noddy inside.

'I think maybe I'll take a look round the place first,' he said.

Noddy gave him a penetrating look. 'Are you short of a pound, boy?' he asked, with a suddenness that startled David into admission.

'It'll be all right, though,' he prevaricated. 'I can get some from the Post Office on Monday. I've got my book with me.'

'What I'm wonderin' is, can you do a bit of nettin'?' Noddy asked.

David had learned to net on the *Silver Spray* and considered himself fairly adept at it.

'You can patch a creel for us?'

'I'm no expert but I patched a few for Donald when I was with him.'

Noddy seemed satisfied. 'Aye, well, I daresay you can make yourself useful to us if you like to come out with us next week. Here, take this.' He pulled a pound note from his wallet and pushed it into David's hand. 'You can pay me it back when you get your own.'

'I'll do that,' said David, feeling himself grow warm with embarrassment and appreciation.

'Okay then. Come inside. What time you spend outside a pub on a Saturday is wasted time.'

The bar was seething with men. Elderly men in dungarees, young men in jeans; men wearing cloth caps or the woollen hats that were known locally as 'Toories' because it was the tourists coming to the port who had originally brought the fashion. Everyone wore thick knitted sweaters, navy-blue ones mostly or else the speckled grey and white that reminded David of the speckled hens his grandmother had once kept. Although it was only a little after eight o'clock there was the urgency of imminent closing time about the way everyone called for their drinks and in the chiding of the barman into haste.

Noddy and David pushed their way to the bar, Noddy waving off offers of drinks and David responding to cautious greetings from those who thought they should know him. The barman pushed a double whisky in front of him and another at Noddy.

'Where's Brad?' shouted Noddy above the noise. 'Can anybody tell me where is Brad?' To David he added, 'He'll have a good drink on him by this time but I'd best tell him what's happenin' while he's still got his senses.'

'Haven't seen him since he came off the boat.' A voice from a huddled group supplied the information without identifying itself.

'He's away down the line.' A small man with one wall eye and a florid scar beneath the other detached himself from another group and made his way towards the bar.

'Down the line?' echoed Noddy disapprovingly.

'Aye, so he is,' a freckle-faced youth affirmed as he selected a fraction of elbow room on the counter. 'I mind seein' him myself all toffeed up goin' into the station.' The youth gulped down most of his glass of whisky. 'He's off to his fancy woman,' he added with a leer.

'I'll give him fancy woman if he's not back in time for Monday mornin',' threatened Noddy.

'Why wouldn't he be back?' demanded the youth. 'He'll be right sick of her before it's Monday.'

'You'd think there'd be enough of his Instant Promise girls here to satisfy him,' grumbled Noddy.

'Ach, not Brad. He's been round the lot of them that many times he's fair scunnered. He's wantin' somethin' fresh,' said the man with the wall eye as he chortled into his whisky.

'I'm thinkin' his fancy woman's fresh enough, then.' The remark came in a placid baritone from a great black-haired bull of a man who stood in the open doorway. Immediately the conversation in the bar was muted.

'You'd know right enough,' muttered the wall-eyed man in a voice that was undeniably envious.

The big man came forward, darting him a whimsical glance and then with a smile settling comfortably on the wrinkles of his face he leaned on a portion of the counter which had suddenly become vacant and gave his attention to the rows of bottles behind the bar.

In common with most people David had a tendency to impose features on characters he had heard described, and during the time he had spent on the *Silver Spray* the fo'c'sle yarnings had included pawky descriptions of almost every inhabitant of the port. 'Pie'—pious Willy, 'terrible wild when he has a good drink on him but when he's sober he says grace to a cup of tea'; David imagined him to be tall and thin with dark restless eyes. 'Jim Tarry, that feeble he ruptured himself boiling an egg for his breakfast'—obviously the concave and pallid type. 'Tom Canty—that mean he wouldn't give a worm to a blind hen'; he envisaged him as being small and broad with eyelids like blinkers and a round, puffy face. There was a whole gallery of characters that had stuck in his mind but the one who had struck him with most awe and had remained most vividly in his memory was that of 'Big Cam'. 'King Herring' was another name they had for him and because he so exactly fitted the mental image he had conceived of him and because of the air of tangible authority which now seemed to make itself felt in the bar David guessed that the big man who had just entered was indeed the 'King' himself.

David recalled the various observations he had heard:

'You'll never see any of his herrin' goin' for fishmeal,' it was claimed.

'Always the best prices for any fish he brings in.' There had been both irony and respect in the voice.

'Aye, but doesn't he always get the best catches, too?' questioned someone else with an air of perplexity.

'An' why wouldn't he?' was the response. 'The bloody herrin's too scared not to go into his nets, that's what it is. It's like as though he hypnotises them.'

Noddy spoke out of the side of his mouth confirming David's guess. 'I'll tell Big Cam who you are,' he said. 'He'll want to know, likely.' He tapped the big man's shoulder.

'This is the chap that was with Donald in the *Silver Spray* back in the spring, you mind him?'

The big man turned to assess David.

'He's comin' out with us next week,' explained Noddy, with it seemed to David a trace of defiance.

'Aye?' said Big Cam. 'I mind fine seein' him. At the lobsters for a time, were you not?' His ice-blue gaze did not melt as he thrust out a hand to shake David's. 'I don't mind what they called you, though,' he added. David was on the point of introducing himself but the big man went on: 'I don't mind what they called you,' he repeated, 'but I know fine what I'm goin' to call you.'

David waited, convinced that his Welsh accents had earned for him the inevitable 'Taffy'. Big Cam's hand still held his. 'I'm pleased to meet you, Beardie,' he said, giving David's hand another shake. His words and action were an accolade and after a fractional silence while the company awaited David's reaction there was a murmur of approving laughter. And so, 'Beardie' he became, from that night on.

He found another double whisky in front of him and the barman answered his look of enquiry with an almost imperceptible nod towards Big Cam. There followed another whisky and then another.

'Here, Beardie.' Big Cam leaned towards him. 'You can tell me somethin', now. Did you ever find yourself sufferin' from sore throats?'

'No,' David replied cautiously. 'Not since I was a child.'

'There now,' said Big Cam. 'That would seem like the proof of it.' He nudged the man on his other side.

'Proof of what?' asked David, mystified.

'Well now,' explained Big Cam. 'I knew a fellow once that used to suffer terrible from sore throats every winter. And the doctor tells him, "You grow a beard man, that'll cure you." Well, he took the doctor's advice and grew a good beard on him and from that day he never had a sore throat since. What do you make of that, now?'

'That'll be the answer to it,' responded the man on his other side.

Noddy grasped David's shoulder. 'Come over a minute while I tell Eggo you're bunkin' with us,' he said and led David to the other end of the bar.

'Come here, you bugger!' he yelled at a short, stumpy, red-headed youth who immediately detached himself from his companions and elbowed his way to them. 'This here is Beardie,' shouted Noddy above the upsurge of noise. 'He's bunkin' aboard tonight and comin' out with us for the trip next week.'

'Good enough,' replied Eggo, shaking David's hand. He insisted on seeing each of them provided with another drink before rejoining his cronies.

'Eggo's the right shape for a fisherman,' Noddy confided, appraising Eggo's back. 'He's short in the leg and weighty behind; that's the sort of figure you need on a boat. It makes for solidness when you're haulin' ropes and means you can reach down without much bendin'.'

'I'm afraid those aren't my strong points,' David confessed with mock apology, looking down at his own long legs and hitching his belt over slim hips and flat stomach.

'No,' conceded Noddy, belching affectionately into his drink. 'No more than mine, but you look as if you can fairly do a day's work all the same.' He looked at David enquiringly.

'I can,' David asserted confidently.

He had to insist on his turn to buy them drinks but by the time they had arrived Noddy had wandered away to join an arguing group in the opposite corner. A few minutes later he was back again with a full glass in his hand. He grasped David's arm firmly.

'Jush a minute, now, Beardie,' he began. 'Wait you while I say somethin'.' His head was tilted backwards so that he could focus his eyes without the strain of lifting his eyelids too high. His voice slithered over the consonants.

'I'm listening,' David said, fearing that Noddy had changed his mind about taking him to sea.

Noddy seemed to be trying to recollect himself. His grip on David's arm relaxed momentarily. 'I just want to say good night to you now and wish you a comfor . . . a . . . bloody good night on board and hopin' you'll find all you want.

Good night. See you Monday.' He breathed solicitously over David.

'You're going already?' David was surprised, remembering Noddy's pronouncement just before they had entered the bar.

'Me? By God, no!' Noddy's tone and expression were full of reproof. Indignation steadied his eyes for a few brief seconds, and his grip of David's arm tightened again as his body swayed backwards. 'I'll be here till they chuck me out, boy,' he elucidated proudly, 'but by then I'll be too drunk to know who you are, never mind to say good night to you, so I'm sayin' it now while I'm still sober.'

David smiled with relief and Noddy lurched away. A moment later Eggo tapped his shoulder, indicating another drink awaiting his attention on the counter.

'My God, but that man fairly takes a drink,' commented Eggo admiringly with a gesture towards Noddy.

With the change in his pocket reduced to a few coppers David thrust his way through the crowd and into the open air. It was dark now and he leaned against a telegraph pole strategically placed outside the pub. His mind was full of drowsy conflict. One half of it urging him just to slouch where he was, the other half insisting that he put his legs to the test and make his way down to the boat. He heard the voices of skylarking children, the ring of a pebble against an oildrum. A large black dog loped towards him, stopped to sniff at his trouser leg and not distinguishing it from the pole abstractedly lifted its leg. He yelled at it but it was too late. A woman's voice called a shocked reprimand. The woman came into the patch of light from the bar windows and he saw that it was Bessie from the tea-shop. She carried the dog's lead in her hand. She paused and called the dog again.

David watched her, a bitter expostulation on his lips.

'I hear you're sleepin' aboard the *Fair Lassie*,' she said, and smiled.

'Aye, maybe,' he grunted incoherently.

'You'll get a proper bed up at our own place if you want it,' she invited and then added quickly, 'It's just myself and my mother that's there.'

Good God! David thought to himself, if you've a mother living she must be a bit of a relic. He said hurriedly, 'No, no, thanks all the same. I'm seeing the boys again tonight yet and it'll be kind of late by the time I'm ready to bunk.'

A man's voice called, 'Aye, aye, Bessie,' and a shaft of light played on her as the pub door swung open. David saw that she was smiling at him with a wide, artless smile that had brought a glow to her still youthful skin. Her eyes looked lustrous.

'Just as you like,' she said, dismissing him. 'Cheerio!'

He watched her disappear into the gloom, asking himself if Noddy's opinion of her was a slanderous one. He thought, regretfully, that he hadn't had much experience of whores.

The dog's urine soaking through his trousers brought disgust and with it a degree of sobriety. He harnessed his muscles and finding them reasonably compliant made his way towards the pier.

There was more light over the water than there had been in the village, and he found his rucksack still where he had left it. The tide had come up so that the lower weed-slimed steps were no longer exposed. Facing the steps, he negotiated them on his hands and knees. As soon as his foot landed on the deck of the nearest boat his mind cleared and with mounting confidence he progressed from deck to deck until he was aboard the *Fair Lassie*. Her fo'c'sle was forrard and he pushed back the hatch cover. Taking the torch from his rucksack he played its beam down into the darkness before descending. He found the light-switch on the deckhead and flicked it on.

The fo'c'sle contained two upper bunks and one lower one on each side, six bunks in all, though one of the lower ones was stuffed with oilskins, tattered books and magazines. The bunks were shallow and narrow—so narrow that a fat man would have been held in one like a vice. Low lockers ran along below the bunks on either side with a folding table between them.

David closed the hatch before he slipped off his trousers. He would leave dipping them over the side until tomorrow, he told himself, for once in the safety of the fo'c'sle the woolly feeling had returned and he was no longer sure of his balance. Suddenly, as he stood there surveying his fouled trousers, wild exultant laughter began to take possession of him. It throbbed in his stomach, heaved in his chest and burst out from his throat unconstrainedly. His knees weakened and he collapsed at last on to a locker. What if a dog had pissed on him? It was possible that in these parts it would be regarded as a token of good luck in much the same way the shitting of a seagull would have been. Nothing mattered. He was back on a boat, wasn't he? No matter how short-lived his stay he was for a time back on a boat with a deck beneath his feet and all the cleanness and unpredictability of the sea around him.

When the laughter had abated he climbed into one of the top bunks. It fitted him like a coffin, leaving no room for restlessness; the blankets smelled of mildew and he pushed them down so that they covered only his bare legs. His pull-over would provide sufficient warmth for his top half. The deckhead light was still on and he wondered if, in the interests of battery economy, he ought to get out and switch it off. He wanted to leave it on to help him wrestle with the in-exorability of sleep; so that he could prolong the time he had to savour all the evidence of this man's world which now enclosed him. Would leaving the light on result in his being cursed for draining the battery when the crew turned up on the Monday morning? He strove with himself, trying to will his legs to swing themselves out of the bunk and take him to the light-switch. The boat rocked him gently like a cradle; the mordent trill of the water against the planking was the sweetest of lullabies. The light became diffused; his eyelashes were imprinted against the glare; debate melted into unconsciousness.

Chapter 3

Waking to the circles of daylight that were the portholes was for David an immediate ecstasy that was only slightly marred by the collision between his head and the top of the bunk as he rose too quickly. He lay back, squinting at the proximity of the deckhead, and revelled again in the knowledge that he was the sole occupant of the fo'c'sle of a seagoing fishing boat moored in a Sabbath-quiet harbour; that he was back in the West of Scotland and that, as it was a Sunday, there was no need to fret about time. There was no sound of wind in the rigging but the boat was exercising herself in an uncertain roll that told him either of a flooding tide or of a sea running outside the harbour. From the other boats there came the noise of rubbing fenders, sounding like the grunting conversation of old men, with every now and then a squeal of protest as two rubbing-bands rasped together and then slid apart. Closer there was the occasional snatch of a chain through a fairlead and closer still, directly above his head, the flip-flap of webbed feet on the deck. The gull seemed to have found something to roll as if it were playing with a toy and he wondered sleepily what it could be. The noise continued tantalisingly until he dismissed it as the sound of its beak nibbling along the seams of the deck. Other gulls made their presence known, not by their practised screams and squawls but by bated mutterings and chatterings, as if the restraint of the Sabbath day had affected them also.

He slept again and when he opened his eyes for the second time the deckhead light appeared brighter, as if daylight had receded rather than advanced. He resolved to bestir himself and turning in his bunk saw with astonishment the three cardboard boxes, no doubt containing the week's supplies, on the opposite locker. They must have been there when he had come aboard last night, he realised, but in his whisky-bemused state their presence had not registered strongly enough to stay in his mind through sleep.

'There'll be food and to spare aboard, so help yourself,' he remembered Noddy telling him some time during the previous evening. Involuntarily he found himself guessing at their contents. Bread, obviously; tea, sugar, butter, jam, condensed milk, bacon and eggs. The thought of the last two items brought the saliva to his mouth and hunger tore at his insides. Rolling out of his bunk he started to pull at the cluster of half-hitches that fastened the first of the boxes. It was bursting with bread—at least a dozen large wrapped loaves, he estimated. The sheer bulk of it made him raise a quizzical eyebrow. He opened the second box. What the hell? How big was the crew of this boat anyway? he asked himself. And how long were they expecting to be at sea? 'Food and to spare', Noddy had said. It struck David as being a supreme understatement. Could three human bellies cope with all that stuff in the five and a half days they would be away from the port? The folded invoice lay on the top and he scanned along the length of the first page, mouthing each item in a loud whisper so as to convince himself he was not exaggerating. Four pounds of butter; four pounds of lard; five pounds of bacon; four dozen eggs; four pounds of tea; twelve pounds of sugar; eight tins of meat; four jars of jam; four swiss rolls; five tins of fruit; six packets of biscuits. The list continued on to a second page and still the quantities of each item seemed to him enormous. It was with something like awe that he investigated the third box to find himself confronted by a prodigious mound of sausages, a couple of cartons of dripping and various chunks of meat that looked substantial enough to feed the whole fishing fleet instead of just the three men who comprised Noddy's crew. If he hadn't seen the boys lugging similar boxes on to each of the other boats the previous day David might have suspected that Noddy was acting as a supply boat for the rest of the fleet. Scratching his head he pondered how three men could dispose of ten pounds of fat in a week, apart from anything else.

Gloating at the prospect of helping them, he turned his attention to the galley stove. It was a typical ship's stove with ring and plates in the top and an oven at the back, and like any unlit, uncleaned stove anywhere it looked thoroughly dispirited. Spurning his first three attempts to light it, it responded to the fourth by filling the fo'c'sle with smoke before it started to burn sluggishly. David grabbed the bucketful of cold ash and cinders he had cleaned out of it and throwing back the hatch carried it up on deck. The rough pungent smells of the harbour were muted by a thin drizzle of rain that was drifting in from the sea, polishing the grey decks of the boats and settling mistily on the draped nets. David tipped the bucket into the harbour and immediately a gull that had been observing him with only fractional interest from the stemhead of the adjoining *Sapphire* swooped towards the dusty ripples, then as if in outrage at his cheating circled round and extruded prodigally along the length of the *Fair Lassie*'s forepeak. He swore at it and reached for a brush, remembering Donald's grumbling when, after being forced to spend a weekend in this same port, they had emerged from their bunks on the Monday morning to find the side-decks of the *Silver Spray* mottled with the ordure of gulls.

'The bloody gulls here,' he had complained bitterly. 'They have nothing else to do on Sundays but shit. They eat that much on Saturdays, what with all the fish offal and the stores being ditched and everything, they just have to shit all day

Sundays so as to make room for the next week's food. It was just the same with my Uncle Hamish,' he had continued. 'He used to go fishing each day in his own little boat and he was that keen to get out he never took anything but a cup of tea and a bowl of brose for his breakfast. That would last him till he got home at night and then he'd be too tired to take more than another cup of tea and more brose. His wife was one of these "wee frees" and she wouldn't let Hamish go fishing on Saturdays because it was too near the Sabbath. She wouldn't cook him a dinner on Sundays either, so every Saturday Hamish used to eat like a shark, to make up for the rest of the week. Then on Sunday morning's he'd be off to the moors and he'd squat there with his pants down and a bible across his knees until it was time for him to go to church in the evening. All weathers, he was out there. He used to make a tent round himself with his oilskin and, honest, you'd hear the groaning coming from under it for a mile off.'

David stood on the deck, facing into the breeze, letting the cold drizzle chase away the last vestiges of his muzzy head. It felt as clean and antiseptic as a wash with carbolic soap. He would have liked to know the time but short of seeing someone to hail there seemed little prospect of finding out. He had flogged his own watch to pay his fare and the alarm clock in the fo'c'sle had stopped at ten minutes to four. He guessed it must be somewhere around ten o'clock but it might just as easily be eight or even twelve. So far as he could see there was no flicker of activity on the shore—not even a smoking chimney. The village seemed to be sleeping still, lulled by the quiet rain, relaxed under the wardship of the mist-screened hills. Like boarding-house guests who had been locked breakfastless out of the dining-room the gulls queued along the ridging of every white-splashed roof while the village slept on. Once again David recalled Donald's succinct description of the life of a fisherman:

'Mondays to Fridays,' he had observed, 'he takes his boat

to sea, Saturdays he takes his thirst to a pub and Sundays he takes his wife to bed. And by God!' he had added, 'by the time Monday morning's come round his wife is that sick of him she's as pleased as the seagulls to get him off to sea again.'

David stretched, filling his lungs with deep counted breaths of fresh air, letting gladness surge through him. He peered down the hatch. The smoke had cleared and the fire was burning with a steady roar so that the smell of hot iron was now added to the compounded smells of oil and mildew, wood and tar of the fo'c'sle. He went below, eager to fill his belly with bacon and eggs.

It was not until he began to unwrap one of the parcels of bacon that he noticed the message scrawled on the wrapper. It was in pencil and read: *B. I think you're great. See you at the dance on Saturday. Love M.* There followed a score or so of 'X's. On a sugar packet he found a similar loving message, though it looked to be in a different hand, and a plethora of 'X's decorated several other items. David decided that 'B' was obviously Brad, who appeared to be a very popular young man with the lassies. He grinned down into the sizzling frying-pan. It looked as if the village girls were a pretty forthcoming lot, anyway, he thought. And not being all that bad-looking himself he could surely look forward to some pleasant diversion himself before very long.

Before very long. He sucked in his breath. That was going to be the snag. How long could he hang on here without being thought a bum? Not, he thought, until Donald was fit for fishing again. 'Come out with us for the week,' Noddy had invited offhandedly, and if he didn't get under everyone's feet too much the week might stretch to a couple, maybe three. But serious fishermen do not take kindly to spare bodies cluttering up their boats. He'd learned that lesson during the few weeks he had been on the *Silver Spray*, and Donald, heaven knew, was only intermittently serious about anything. He resolved to keep his ears and eyes open and his legs nifty enough to make himself useful—useful enough to be offered a berth if and when one became available.

Full of breakfast, his stomach warm inside and out, he climbed out of the fo'c'sle and across the boats on to the pier, revelling in the sight of the waiting fleet ready at the casting of a rope and the flick of a switch to throb its questing way to the fishing grounds. The drizzle was heavier now and he blinked it from his eyelashes and wrung it from his beard with a squeeze of his hand. The mist had crept in low over the land so that parts of the houses were poised like disembodied fragments—a roof here, a gable there. The pier was cut off from the village by a bank of mist and even if there were signs of life he was not now able to discern them. He sought the lavatory in the station waiting room and then went back to the *Fair Lassie*. Back again in the fo'c'sle he spotted an opened packet of cigarettes lying on one of the bunks and with a vague recollection of having bought them himself the previous evening he took out a cigarette. Putting more coal on the stove and adjusting the damper so that it burned slowly he shut the hatch and sat down on a locker, intent on sorting out the incidents of the last few days; on coming to grips with this bug which, since his initiation with Donald earlier in the season, had bitten deep into him, filling him with restlessness and discontent; engendering in him an urgent desire to have done with the nine-to-five boredom of his job in which only the prospect of an evening's chase round on his old B.S.A. had got him through each day; and only the contemplation of a fine weekend when, with haversack and climbing gear, he could take himself off to the hills, had got him through each week. He could not account for his sudden recognition of the desire to be on the sea. None of his forbears had ever had the remotest connection with the sea and yet, when he had stepped aboard the *Silver Spray* that day so many months ago now, he had felt a tingling in his veins that was like the first recognition of a love affair. The sea then had been brisk, decorated with chevrons of spume, and he had sat out the whole trip on the forepeak, insulated by his state of enchantment from the slapping of the cold spray and the derision of his comfortably ensconced companions.

The four of them, all members of the local climbing club, had planned to spend this, their first holiday in Scotland, in tackling as many peaks as they could climb in the two weeks that were allotted to them for their annual vacation. To save themselves the exacting task of carrying all their gear across the long stretch of bog and rock which was the only land route, Donald and his *Silver Spray* had been commissioned to take them by sea to the encampment at the foot of the hill which was scheduled to be their first climb. By the time they had unloaded their stuff, watched the *Silver Spray* turn from the quiet anchorage to head for home and had pitched their tents, a mist had come swirling in from the sea, swift and silent, chill and damp. They had been glad to cook up a meal on the primus and then crawl into their sleeping bags, resolved to get a good night's sleep and be ready to start with the dawn in the morning.

When they woke and ventured outside the tents the mist was still enveloping them. It was a warmer mist now, full of midges that attacked every inch of exposed flesh and even penetrated under their eyelids and inside their ears. The aggressors invaded the tents once the flaps were open and despite a barrage of cigarette smoke continued to torment them until they were all exacerbated with the discomfort. Except for snatched meals they had spent most of that day shrouded in their sleeping bags, smoking as they discussed proposed routes though so far they had done no more than glimpse the peaks of the hills.

Just before darkness fell the mist and the midges had been cleared by a breeze that at first had only skated over the lazy ripples in the anchorage but during the night had increased to gale force, funnelling through the hills and bringing with it torrential rain. A sudden forceful downdraught had flattened their tents around them and though they strove to re-erect them they soon realised that the light canvas was tearing.

Conceding victory to the weather they had bundled the tents up in the shelter of a crag and climbing into their sleeping bags they had spent the night in the open. When morning came they had had to search morosely for an hour or so before they found all the parts of their primus which had been scattered along with the rest of their stores over half a mile of heather and bog. They had retrieved everything eventually, except for a tube of suntan cream which David was sure had been among his kit. But no one even suggested looking for that.

The wind had abated though there were still rain showers and they decided to try a short climb that day just to get the feel of the hills. High up, though, the wind became too gusty and threatening for them to attempt anything more ambitious and they had returned disconsolately to their tents.

During the ensuing three days the skies had seemed intent on bombarding them with a sample of every kind of foulness they had in their arsenal. Hailstones as big as cherries hit them with a sudden fury as they were crossing a steep exposed slab; a funnel of wind almost lifted David off his feet when he was doing a difficult traverse. They were at the mercy of falling stones dislodged by the heavy rain, and lightning caused them more than once to abandon a climb. Their leader became moodier as time went by and they had attained only the first of their objectives, and that only by the endurance of more than an acceptable measure of discomfort. Gloomily they mooched around the lower hills or lay in their tents, yarning, joking, eating and sleeping, while they waited for the weather to improve. Then to crown it all, their leader, though as lissom on a precipice as a ballet dancer, went down to the anchorage one morning to empty some rubbish, slipped on the weedy rocks and hurtled forward into the water. When he came out he had lost his thick-lensed spectacles without which he was unable to see a rope five feet in front of his nose.

'My luck's out,' he said glumly. 'I'll have to make tracks for home.'

'I'll come with you,' one of the others volunteered.

They had talked things over together and admitting that they were competent but not dedicated climbers decided there would probably be just as much satisfaction in spending the remainder of their holiday in the hills nearer home where at this time of year there was not likely to be such inclement weather to contend with. They had eaten as much of their stores as they could and left the rest in a cache where they might be spotted by future climbers. Then shouldering their equipment they began the long trudge over the moors back to the village where they could catch a bus that would deliver them to the railway station. Descending wearily from the mist-trimmed hills they walked into the remnants of evening sunshine that were touching the sea with gold.

Donald, whose lazy eyes missed nothing, came ambling along to accost them. 'Ach, but I understood you were staying till Friday week,' he greeted them in his gentle Highland brogue.

They told him that the weather and the midges and now their leader's predicament had made climbing too much of a hazard.

'Aye, that's bad right enough,' he admitted. 'But the worst of the weather's over, I'm thinkin'. Look at that, now!' He gestured towards the islands that lay crouched against a bruised but tranquil sky. 'There's no more wind up there, d'you see? Not for a day or two, anyway. You've given up just a day too soon for we're surely in for a fine spell of weather now.'

He sounded so confident that it was possible the weather

would not have the heart to betray his prophecy.

'You're due for it,' said the spectacle-less leader, from whom the weather portents were screened by the mist of his own short-sightedness. 'I was beginning to doubt if you ever had good weather in these parts.'

Donald winced as if the remark were a personal affront.

David nodded towards the hills they had left. 'It doesn't look much better over there yet, anyway,' he pointed out.

'Aye, well, it always takes a wee bitty longer for it to clear in the hills,' Donald said, looking sadly at the dark piled clouds which still gloated over the peaks.

David's grunt was touched with irony.

'I was wonderin',' Donald began as they prepared to pitch their tents for the night, 'would one of you give me a hand to pull down my boat. The tide's right out and I was thinkin' maybe you could do with a fish for your supper.'

David volunteered immediately. He was yet to learn that Donald was always on the lookout for a helping hand and that subsequently that hand found itself doing most of the work.

'So you're thinkin' of goin' back,' he said to David as they trudged over the shingle towards the dinghy. 'It's a pity, that.' Between them he and David launched the dinghy in the shallow water. Donald got in and then indicating a handleless pail and a piece of cord which lay on an oildrum further up the shore asked David to bring them for him. 'Would you no' fancy comin' fishin' for an hour?' he invited.

David hesitated only for a fraction of a second, looking back to where his friends were busy about the tents. They could manage without him, he decided. He made to step into the dingy but Donald had, it seemed unintentionally, let the boat drift out a yard or two from the shore.

'Them boots is awful heavy for my wee boat.' He back-watered with an oar and pointed with a regretful grimace to

David's climbing boots. 'Would you not take them off? You'll not find it cold without them.'

David took his boots off, dumped them at the top of the tide and in his stockinged feet slithered over the wet stones back to the dinghy.

'Now, see will you take the oars and we'll go out to the boat while I put this bitty rope on the pail, just.' Donald sat facing David with the pail between his knees, intent on tying the rope in a barrel knot around its rim. 'You can row?' he asked, as an afterthought.

'I could once,' David admitted. He felt flustered, and reluctant to tell Donald that his only experience of boats had been on the boating pool at a seaside resort where the Sunday School had gone for its annual treat. He had spent all his pocket money that day trying to make the boat respond to the oars and then trying to perfect his manipulation of them so that his pulling became rhythmic and smooth. Unfortunately the Sunday School had not been able to afford another trip to the seaside in David's time and the scholars had had to be content with a bunfight and games on the local football field.

The first few strokes he pulled splashed a lot of water over Donald, but he only smiled and looked over David's shoulder to check that his steering was good enough.

'Pull on your left oar and get her round,' he advised as the dinghy moved nearer to where the *Silver Spray* lay still at her moorings. David pulled on his left oar but as they came alongside he forgot to ship the other so that if Donald had not snatched it from the rowlock the blade would have smashed between the two boats.

'Sorry,' mumbled David.

'That was no' bad at all,' was Donald's only comment, and he made it seem like a compliment. David did not know then as he came to know later that if Donald paid you a compliment it was only a way of memorising an incident so that he could truthfully include his own comment in the narrative when the time came to relate it—which would not be when the victim was around.

The loch was ruffled with evening wind as the *Silver Spray* nosed her way purposefully towards a long spur of land in the lee of which they were to fish. When the engine stopped at last the drum of snipe came intermittently through the rumble of surf that was breaking and cascading lazily over the rocks of the shore. To David the rocks looked too close for comfort but Donald seemed happy enough. He handed David a 'darra' —a dozen or so hooks attached to a length of gut in turn attached to a bundle of line wrapped round and round a hand-sized chunk of cork. An old spanner did duty as a sinker. Donald gave David some brief instructions on how to use it.

'What about bait?' David queried. He knew very little about fishing but he could see that there had been feathers attached to some of the darra hooks. Now all that remained of the feathers was their bald shards.

'You'll not be needin' bait for mackerel if it's here,' Donald told him. 'They're just waitin' to commit suicide.' He unrolled his own tackle, and threw it out over the side. Treating the bristling hooks with caution David lowered his darra into the water and unwound a few fathoms of line from the cork until the lead hit the bottom, or what he thought was the bottom. Following Donald's instructions he pulled in a stretch or two to keep the lead out of the weed-enjungled rocks. With a suddenness that momentarily stunned him with surprise the line started to drag swiftly through his fingers and with instant assessment of the situation he put his foot on the cork before it too was pulled over the side. It was incredible. Utterly and completely unbelievable! But even before Donald had turned to him with wide, excited eyes and a shout of 'It's solid!' he realised that the lead had not touched bottom at all but had landed on a shoal of fish so tight packed that there was not an inch of space for the lead to penetrate it. The next few moment were so hectic that David could not stop to count the fish that were on the darra each time he pulled it out of the water. He was only aware of the line breaking surface with a scintillating fish on every hook; of Donald swearing as he planted a gumbooted foot on the tangle of gut that was momently becoming more inextricable as the fish writhed and leaped in the bottom of the boat; of exuberant joy alternating with the cursing of his own inexpert and now bloody fingers as he tore the mackerel off the hooks; of Donald hauling in his own line and bounding from tiller to engine between rushes of helping him to unhook more and yet more fish; of almost losing his foothold as the bottom boards became deep with fish and coated with their scales and slime. In regaining his balance he had trodden on a fish-hook which had dug deep into his unshod foot; and Donald seeing what had happened, had rushed forward, concerned not for his plight but to break the hook from the darra so that there should be no interruption of the fishing. There had come a moment of tension then when Donald had suddenly looked up with panic in his face and simultaneously David had become aware of the pounding swell very, very near at hand. A gull screamed at them as it took off from its roost on the cathedral-grand rocks that were looming almost close enough for them to touch. The engine was revved fiercely and *Silver Spray* churned the water astern as she backed away. They made again for safe water but though they tried several depths with the darras the mackerel proved unresponsive.

'I'm thinkin' we've lost them,' said Donald resignedly, 'but ach, I daresay we have plenty.'

They both looked down at the couple of hundred fish in the bottom of the boat, moribund now but still with a gaping mouth, a fluttering gill or a quivering tail showing itself here and there. Their rainbow glistening was smudged with bloody stains.

'Do you often get fishing like this?' David asked bemusedly.

'Plenty times, if you know where to look and the right time to look,' said Donald with a shrug of his shoulders. He throttled down the engine again. 'You'll take the tiller now and I'll try will I get a drag with the eel,' he invited authoritatively.

'I'd like to have this hook out first,' David insisted and thrust his foot towards Donald.

'Aye, aye.' Competently Donald worked at the hook and extracted it. 'Stick your foot over the side for a wee whiley,' he suggested. 'You'll take no harm so long as you have it in sea water.'

So while Donald trailed the rubber eel and the *Silver Spray* cruised slowly along David sat astride the stern, one hand on the tiller, his sore foot in the water. His body was still vibrant with the thrill of his night's experiences and he could not stop himself from glancing again and again down at the silver harvest which now gaped and twitched no more. The engine throbbed quietly like the heartbeat of the night.

Donald kicked several of the fish from under the seats where they had writhed themselves to and then, still with a keen eye on the line that trailed in the water, he took out his knife, picked up some of the larger fish and slitting their silver bellies threw the guts into the water. David also took out his knife and picked up a mackerel. Colourfully the guts oozed out, the gall bladder a beautiful translucent shade of green. He remarked, 'What glamorous guts these fishes have.'

Donald looked at him uncomprehendingly for a moment, then replied: 'Aye, but it doesn't stop the buggers stinkin' if you leave them in too long.' He put his knife away. 'That'll be enough for the house,' he said. 'They're not over-keen on the mackerel. The rest'll go for bait so we don't need to gut them.'

He slumped back into his seat and gave a tentative pull or two on the line. His patient eyes contemplated the polished line of sea, puckered with the dark shapes of islands that were still clearly definable against the hybrid night sky of these northern parts. David stared reflectively at the water as if he was beginning to see his dreams. A swift flash astern roused him and he turned to see Donald hauling in the line, steadily, hand over hand. There was a gleam of silver in the water beside the boat; a splashing as the fish was drawn up. It was a lythe about eighteen inches long. A splendid fish, David thought, but Donald only gave him a fleeting grin and threw it with a dissatisfied air on top of the piled mackerel. He let out the line again and not until there were half a dozen fish of similar size did he suggest going home.

There was only one dim light showing in the village as they moored up the *Silver Spray* and climbed once again into the dinghy.

'You'd best come up to the house and take a cup of tea,' Donald said as they rowed ashore. Before answering David looked over to where the two tents of his companions had been pitched for the night. There was no light or sound from them.

'I ought to get back and get some shut-eye,' he said indecisively.

They hauled the dinghy up the shore and David sat on a stone while he pulled on his heavy boots. 'That bus leaves at seven in the morning, doesn't it?'

'Aye, seven or thereabouts,' agreed Donald indifferently. 'If you're goin' to catch it then it's no' much use your botherin' to go to bed at all,' he went on. 'It must be well at the back of three now.'

'Three!' David ejaculated, realising that he had been lulled by the deceptive night. Hastily he took out his watch. It assured him that it was indeed twenty minutes past three.

'You'll need a bite to eat before you go,' Donald said. 'So you'd best come up to the house and have something.'

Through the rustling, sea serenaded night they walked to his cottage which proved to be the one where the light still burned. Donald turned up the wick of the lamp. The room was austere; wooden chairs; lineoleum-covered table and a workaday dresser crammed with pottery. The stove was a modern all-night burning one, however, and as soon as Donald pulled out the damper there was a responsive roar in the chimney. He pushed a pan and a kettle on to the hotplate and then turned to root in a cupboard from which he produced a bottle of whisky and a couple of glass tots. By the time they had swallowed a couple of drams the soup in the pan was bubbling and the kettle was gushing steam. They broke thick hunks of bread into the soup and spooned greedy mouthfuls. Then with cups of tea and cigarettes they tilted back their chairs, put their feet on the stove and prepared themselves to yarn the rest of the night away.

The ringing of an alarm clock in the room above them made David jump and he realised that he must have dozed off. 'Time I went to join the boys,' he said.

'An' that's how it is,' Donald said, as if he was finishing off a story. 'With him away to Glasgow I'll just have to manage by myself.'

David became guiltily conscious that Donald had been telling him of some predicament he was in and that his drowsiness had caused him to miss the importance of the story. He asked a judicious question or two and elicited that Donald had been bemoaning the loss of his fishing partner who, for the past year, had been helping him fish his creels but who, at last admitting an unconquerable fear of the sea, had gone off to join the police force.

'Can't you get someone else, then?' David asked.

Donald put his cup down on the stove with a despairing gesture. 'Not a one. That's just what I'm after tellin' you. There's nothing but old folks here now. All the young ones go away. Anyway,' he added with what David suspected to be spurious gloom, 'there's no money in fishing lobsters these days. Not unless you do it on a big enough scale.' He shot David a quick look from under his brows as if expecting to be contradicted.

'Too bad,' David commiserated as his eyelids drooped again.

'I'm thinkin',' Donald's voice arrested his desire for sleep. 'If you were still here tomorrow we could go out to the far point and fill the boat with fish. This time of year there's plenty of real fishin' there.'

David blinked, and stared so hard that Donald became embarrassed and got up to poke the fire so that he could turn his back. 'Well, why not?' David mused. He still had a week of his holiday left and it wouldn't make any difference to the boys whether he returned with them or not. He felt flattered and excited at the invitation but he managed to keep his voice from being too enthusiastic as he answered. 'It sounds a good idea,' he said.

It was raining when they went to acquaint his climbing companions with his change of plan. Grey rain clouds sagged on the hills and the sea was stippled with its patterns. It seemed to David that like his own the eyes of the day were still half shut.

The boys were packing up their tents and greeted them with early-morning lugubriousness.

'Thought you said the weather was improving,' one of them taunted Donald.

'Aye, well it will, it will,' Donald insisted.

They accepted David's decision to stay on for another week with Donald with murmurings of surprise.

'You're a glutton for punishment,' they told him, and when the bus jerked itself away up the rough track taking them with it one of them called back, 'Hope you've got plenty of Kwells.'

Donald and David returned to the cottage where David

was introduced to Donald's wife, his mother, his sister and his small son, all of whom seemed to have an equal air of authority in the household. They had a quick breakfast and Donald's wife found for David a yellow oilskin smock that would protect him from the assault of the rain and spray, along with a towel to tuck into its loose neck.

Together he and Donald went out again to the *Silver Spray* and immediately David's initiation into lobster fishing began. He learned how to bait the creels; how to extract the lobsters without risking his fingers getting bitten by their vicious claws. He learned to repair the torn netting of creels that had been mutilated by the jagged rocks beneath the water. In the evenings they fished for bait, salting any surplus away in large barrels against the time when fish should perhaps be scarce or the weather too wild for them to go out.

'When do you sleep at this job?' David asked Donald once.

Donald replied: 'Ach, you just snatch an hour when you feel you need it. When you're gettin' good fishin' you don't seem to need a quarter of the sleep you can't do without when the fishin's poor.'

The weather and consequently the fishing were good all that week and the chances of snatched hours for sleep were few indeed. But David was happier than he had ever been. Even before the week came to an end he had made up his mind to stay on as long as he could. Reproachful letters came from his parents, urging him to return to the job which, in their opinion, offered such excellent prospects, but he could not bring himself to the point of saying goodbye to the buoyant days in the *Silver Spray* and catch the labouring bus which would be the first stage of his journey home. He knew that he would ultimately have to go back if only to earn some money. Donald regarded his work only in the nature of an apprenticeship, giving David his food and a bed but no share of the takings, which he invariably grumbled were meagre enough.

'If you could get a few creels for yourself, now,' he said,

'we could go into partnership and that would mean a pound or two for yourself, maybe.' But creels cost money and David was already down to his last few shillings apart from his fare home. He was down to rolling his own cigarettes, allowing himself a few puffs at a time and then putting it back in his pocket ready for the next smoke.

So for a few weeks his life in the *Silver Spray* continued. When it was too rough to go on the sea he and Donald spent their days beachcombing, bringing back loads of driftwood that might be used for creel bottoms or would burn on the kitchen stove. They found other things too: buckets, rope fenders, netfloats and empty oildrums, most of which they carried home to add to Donald's store. The oildrums gave Donald peculiar satisfaction. He already had a stack of them in the back of an old shed which he always kept safely locked.

'What are you going to do with all that lot?' David teased him. 'Thinking of opening a depot or something?'

Donald replied with great earnestness: 'Ach, you never know in these parts when you're going to need a thing. They could come in useful some day.'

David found himself collecting his own treasures with the avidness of a small boy. A ship's porthole—he planned to fit that into the door of his shed at home; a yachting cap which he might some time wear; sea-urchin shells, tonka beans and pieces of coral that would delight his sister Megan and also remind him of his one-time intimacy with the sea.

It was a letter from Megan that eventually forced his return. The plans for her wedding to the assistant choirmaster at the Horeb Chapel had been well ahead when he had left for his holiday. Now, with only a fortnight to go before the day, she wrote telling David she could not possibly go through with it. She had, she said, confided her reluctance to her fiancé who had in turn disclosed her fickleness to her parents. The shock had made them bitterly indignant but after some discussion all three had resolved to treat her change of mind as nothing but pre-wedding nerves and had refused to countenance any alteration or postponement of the wedding plans. Megan pleaded with David now to return and stand by her in her fight. *I desperately want to talk to you*, she had written, *for something has happened that I can't tell them, so please, please, come back and help me.*

Chapter 4

Donald expressed sorrow at his going but David, sensing that he was apprehensive of the question of a share in the profits again being raised, suspected that his sorrow was tinged with relief. Donald was by no means an ungenerous man except where actual money was concerned, when the parting with even the smallest coin seemed to affect him as much as the infliction of a physical hurt. Had the local shopkeeper been willing he would have got his daily packet of cigarettes on credit and his wife confided to David that she could rarely get a pound out of him for the housekeeping. Her only recourse was to let their bed to boarders in the summer and use the money it brought her. What Donald made, according to her, he kept in some hidey-hole known only to himself. With sudden perception David realised it was very likely packed away in his hoard of oildrums.

So David had returned to his parents' home in Llandan, the Welsh mining town, here he had been born and bred. It was a steep-sloping, slate-grey village, enclosed by wastes of coal-mining and smoke-scoured hills where never a breath of sea air ever penetrated. In fact legend had it that an old sailor, sick at last of the sea and resolving to retire to a spot as far away from it as he could find, had set off from Cardiff, walking in a northerly direction. Over his shoulder he had carried, as a memento, the anchor from his last ship and as he plodded on people looked at him curiously and asked: 'Why are you carrying that anchor over your shoulder when you are so far from the sea?' Ignoring their questions he had continued his journey until he came to Llandan. There the people looked at him curiously and asked: 'What is that thing you are carrying over your shoulder?' At last the sailor knew he had come far enough.

Walking down the familiar street David stopped at the door of his home. With some surprise he noticed that it had been re-painted recently, as had all the front of the house. He pushed open the door and saw that inside too had all been redecor-ated. All ready for the wedding, he thought. He had let no one know he was coming and when, with his rucksack still on his back, he went into the kitchen his mother turned with a start of surprise. Immediately she saw him her face became taut-lipped and hostile.

'What's brought you back, then?' she asked witheringly.

'It's time, isn't it?' he retaliated with an attempt at jaunti-ness.

'Past time.' Her voice was even grimmer than her expres-sion. She was frying fish and the staleness of it was such an affront that he wrinkled his nose. If that smell had been detected on board the *Silver Spray* he and Donald would have been sniffing under the floorboards, swearing that some bait had been dropped and left to stink there.

'I suppose you know you've lost your job?' his mother said.

'I suppose so,' he said indifferently.

'You're nothing but a disgrace,' she began.

'Oh, hell!' he snarled. 'It's started already, has it?'

She raised the fish-slice as if she would like to hit him with it.

'Don't you dare to swear in this house,' she commanded, outrage swelling her breast and edging her voice with dis-cordancy. With a faint shock he realised that it was in fact the first time he had used even the mildest oath in her presence.

'Coming back here and expecting just to walk in and carry on,' she resumed, in full spate. 'We consider you a disgrace to the family.'

He wondered just what she thought he had been up to during the past few weeks.

'You wait till your father comes in,' she threatened. 'He'll put you in your place.'

He escaped from the smell of the fish and her tirade up to his bedroom, hearing her final shaft as he climbed the stairs. 'You're no son of ours any longer, let me tell you!'

Up in his room he was dismayed to find that the bed had been stripped and the room emptied of his belongings with a thoroughness that was more emphatic than any spoken reprimand. 'If thine eye offend thee, pluck it out.' He could almost hear his father's ruthless declamation; could see his mother's swiftly and staunchly abetting him. He went to the window and pulling back a fistful of the precisely hung lace curtain scowled out at the row of drab houses opposite, conscious after these weeks of staring into distance of having to refocus his eyes by their proximity. Beyond the blocks of houses there were glimpses of smouldering bings, pithead machinery, railway yards and tall chimneys pumping smoke into clouds that were already surfeited with grime. He had to peer to discern the outline of the hills which lay beyond.

His mother was right. He could be no son of this house any longer. Before long his father would be home and because his father would believe himself to be aiding the Devil if he allowed David to continue living under his roof they would part in anger. It was inevitable. His mother would be an accessory; her disappointment in David and her faith in her husband's judgment being too strong for her to interfere. It was pathetic, David mused, pathetic and touching, this utter subjection to her husband. She was so proud of his undeviating loyalty to his employers which, after thirty years, had brought him the exalted position of manager in the local ironmongery store; proud of his strong baritone voice which never erupted into anything but hymns; proud of his status at the local Horeb Chapel where he was not only superintendent but also a lay preacher; proud of the fact that he did not drink or smoke or swear or keep pigeons in the loft or have any of the weaknesses of other men. Always throughout David's childhood she had been a silent ally to the frequent chastisements he had received from his father, no matter how trivial his offence may have been. Only once had he heard a whisper of disloyalty escape her lips and that was when, as a boy of eight, he had brought home a puppy which he had rescued from the canal bank. While fishing for tiddlers he had heard faint whimpers coming from an old sack which was lying in some reeds and investigating it he had found the puppy. Someone had obviously bungled the job of drowning it and the poor little mite was soaking wet and shivering with cold and fright. Daringly, and knowing his father's abhorrence of animals anywhere near the house, he had taken it home, smuggling it up to his bedroom where with the connivance of his sister he had warmed it and nursed it, feeding it with bread and milk saved from his own supper. For three days he and Megan had shared the fear and ecstasy of their secret, foolishly letting themselves become more enamoured of the puppy, foolishly persuading themselves they might just be allowed to keep it. On the fourth night, because he had been kept back at bedtime for a lecture from his father after a report that he had snatched a hair ribbon from one of the girls at school, he had been later than usual going upstairs. The puppy had betrayed its presence by a series of delighted yelps. Immediately Megan had burst into the room and together they stood petrified listening to the heavy thud of his father's feet on the stairs. David could feel the muscles at the side of his mouth tense as if he were about to vomit and he clutched the puppy so tightly that it yelped again. With blazing eyes his father strode across the room, snatched the puppy from David in one hand and landed a blow at his head with the other. David fell against Megan and she in turn stumbled against the washstand so that the ewer rattled in the basin. It was not the blow, however, but the patch of coldness left in his arms where the warm bundle of puppy had been that helped him to find his voice.

'Please, Father,' he begged, putting all the entreaty he could manage into his voice. 'Let me keep it.'

His father made no sign that he had heard him and in a panic David rushed at him, pulling at his jacket. His father had lifted a stockinged foot and pushed him away. In that instant a way to retaliate flashed into his mind. Picking up the bible which his father had given to him for a birthday present only a couple of weeks previously, he had flung it at him.

'If you don't let me keep it I'll tear that thing up!' he yelled.

His father had stopped then and turned to stare at the bible where it lay on the floor. His glance came back to David and his white, taut face was terrifying.

'I'll teach you to bring dogs into this house behind my back,' he crackled. 'And I'll teach you to defile the Holy Book.'

David saw his mother standing in the doorway, a hot-water bottle clasped to her, and as his father pushed her out of his way her eyes sought his, imploringly, it seemed, and for one brief, sweet moment David thought she was going to intercede on behalf of the puppy. But she remained silent, letting him go without a gesture. As they heard the outer door close and his brisk hard footsteps going out into the street her hand went up to clutch at the neck of her blouse but still she said nothing. By this time Megan and David had their arms around each other, their mutual comfortings interspersed with deep sobs. Megan was shivering and her mother pulled her away, not ungently, and urged her back to her own bedroom. David was sitting on the bed aching with anguish when his mother returned and he steeled himself for the inevitable reprimand. She only said: 'If it had been just me I might have let you keep it but you knew very well what our dad's like about dogs, didn't you?' David detected a slight tremor in her voice and it was too much for him.

'Go away!' he shouted at her and jumping into bed hunched himself into an impregnable position beneath the clothes. Later, when his father had returned to administer the promised thrashing she did not appear and when, the next morning, he again had to endure his father's still boiling rage, she had stood in her accustomed position behind her husband's chair, silently assuring him of her participation.

That evening Megan had told David tearfully that their father had thrown the puppy back into the canal. For days afterwards they were sullen with grief and David felt himself tingle with hatred every time his father spoke to him. With the resilience of an eight-year-old he survived the experience, though from that night on he was aware of a cold wedge of dislike embedding itself into him. Seeking to make some attempt at revenge he had decided that 'Dad' and 'Mam' were far too companionable names for him to call his parents and with the idea that it sounded more aloof set himself to practise calling them 'Father' and 'Mother'. Even when, after some time, he softened sufficiently to reinstate them among those he habitually asked God to bless in his prayers it was not as 'Mam' and 'Dad' as of old but as 'Mother and Father', reflecting stubbornly that if God didn't choose to recognise them by their new designations then they'd just have to take their chance of being blessed.

When the time had come for David to leave school his father's stern enforcement of discipline had ensured that he went into the cash desk of the ironmongery shop where he was manager. David would have preferred a job on a farm but his parents considered farm work degrading and none of the local farmers, all 'strong for the chapel', would have risked offending them by taking David into their employ. David appreciated that their ambitions for him were modest enough. They hoped only that he would become a model employee at the shop and in course of time make a worthy successor to his father at the chapel.

When he was fifteen it seemed that things might be going as they wished for just then an evangelist came to stir up religious fervour in the village and as he was allotted their spare bedroom David saw quite a lot of him. He was an earnest and dedicated man but for the strait-laced chapel-goers he displayed too much levity in the pulpit. He spiced his sermons with humour and it made them uncomfortable. He had a loud, boisterous laugh which, though he restrained it on Sundays, would burst out during conversations in the village street. David's parents displayed towards him an attitude of cautious respect but David grew both to like and admire the man. By the time his fortnight's stay was over he had cajoled David not only into becoming a teacher at the Sunday School but also into pumping the organ for the evening service instead of going out with the boys. He had begun to think it would indeed be pleasant to be as much respected in the town as his father; that it would be gratifying to go up into the pulpit and have the attention of a chapel full of worshippers who would afterwards cluster round you at the chapel door to compliment you on your excellent sermon. It might be nice too to have his mother look at him with that ineffable look she gave his father when, as sometimes happened, people stopped him in the street to say, 'Oh, but that sermon of yours on Sunday did me good, Mr Jones. Never preached a better one, you haven't.'

But by the time he was seventeen religion had become a troubled doubting and questioning and chapel-going an irritation. Except for anniversaries when he went to hear Megan sing her annual solo he forsook it altogether. At eighteen he had saved up enough money to buy himself a second-hand motor-cycle and thereafter spent his Sundays in tearing noisily over the negotiable parts of the moors in company with other enthusiasts. There were girls too, but though his pillion became permanently indented with the shape of feminine bottoms he could never spare for them the devotion or attention he lavished on his bike. Since deserting the chapel he had come to regard himself as an atheist but then he discovered climbing and up in the mountains he came to recognise an omnipresence that had persistently eluded him within the shiny green walls of the chapel, despite the painted banner above the choir stalls which proclaimed that 'God is with us'.

Life at home grew steadily more strained as their ways diverged although now his parents limited themselves to silent condemnation. With the cynicism of youth he believed it was because they suspected he might leave home if they made things too unpleasant for him and that they feared the consequent loss of his wage packet. Not infrequently he contemplated going off on his own to roam the country trying his luck at any sort of job that came along, but always when he mentioned the idea to Megan she had looked so dismayed at being left alone with their parents that he had always relented, for their loyalty to each other was unaffected by a patent disparity of character and appearance. David was dark and tall and rebellious. Megan was fair and slight with a nature so gentle and submissive that left to herself she would have acquiesced to every plan her parents made for her rather than risk a trace of discord. She exasperated David sometimes with her timidity.

Not until they were twenty-one and Megan, with her parents' complete approval had become engaged to Owen, the assistant choirmaster at the chapel, did David feel he could begin to make plans for his escape. The engagement was scheduled to last for a year and when he had left for his Scottish climbing holiday there had still been over two months to go before the date of the wedding fixed for the middle of August. There had been no doubt then in anyone's mind, least of all his own, that he would be back home in plenty of time. He was appalled now to realise how little he had thought of Megan and her plans while caught up with all the business and enchantment of his sojourn in the north.

Megan came hurrying down the street towards the house and he flicked the curtain to attract her attention. She looked up and the glad smile that swept away her troubled frown made him ashamed of his reluctance to return. He heard her exchange a brief word of greeting with his mother in the kitchen and then she was running upstairs. When she burst into his room she was crying.

'Oh, David!' she sobbed. 'I'm so glad you've come back. I haven't known what to do.'

Chapter 5

He put his arm around her shoulders and the tumbling words came on squeaky breaths punctuated with deep anguished sobs. She just couldn't, she confessed, marry Owen. Oh, there was nothing wrong with him and for a long time she'd thought she'd be happy with him but lately she'd got round to thinking she wasn't the wife for him nor he the man for her. Owen had been very kind when she'd told him but had insisted she should have time to think things over before they changed any of their wedding plans. When he'd found she just grew more miserable he'd gone and talked to Father and Mother. They'd been horrified at the prospect of a scandal. What would people say about her jilting Owen as near to the wedding as this? Why couldn't she have said sooner? And then they had comforted themselves by assuring both Owen and Megan that this change of mind was only a whim, a phase such as all brides go through and that the wedding should not be postponed because of it. Owen had seemed inclined to agree with them and now they would not even listen to her when she insisted she couldn't go through with it.

'You said something else had happened,' David encouraged her.

She dried her eyes and her hands fell into her lap.

'Yes,' she whispered. 'I've met someone I like.'

'Someone you think you're in love with?' he asked gently.

'I don't just think, Dave, I know I'm in love with him.' Her voice was urgent and her tear-bright eyes were swiftly radiant. 'I've never felt like this before, not about Owen, anyway.'

'Who is it, Meg?' he asked. 'Do I know him?'

'He knows you. I don't know if you remember him.' She was twisting the wet handkerchief between her hands.

'Tell me,' he coaxed.

'His name's Harry Welch,' she said, turning to hide her flushed face on his shoulder. 'I met him when he came to paint the house,' she confessed. 'I daresay you've noticed?'

David nodded.

'We just seemed to take a fancy to each other right from the first. We've met a few times since then and we know now that we're in love with each other and want to get married as soon as we can.'

David whistled. 'Just like that?' he asked, and felt rather than saw her confirmation. He was marvelling at the change in her.

'This fellow Harry,' he said. 'He used to be a miner, didn't he?'

'Yes,' she admitted and added hastily, 'But he gave it up for the decorating trade. He's doing well at it.'

'And didn't he do a bit of boxing at one time?'

'He still does.' Megan was pleased that he had remembered that. 'He has a fight about once a month and people say he's pretty good. He's won quite a few prizes anyway so he must be.' She tried to smother the pride in her voice.

'Steady, is he?' David pursued seriously.

'Yes.' She nodded emphatically and then her tone became glum. 'But he does take a drink now and then,' she admitted fearfully.

David whistled again and gave her a keen glance.

'I'm not asking him to give it up,' she said. 'He never takes more than a glass a night and he says it keeps him fit.'

'Well,' David said, beginning to grin. 'You have copped yourself a packet, haven't you, old girl? Have you said anything to Mother and Father yet?'

'I haven't dared,' wailed Megan. 'How could I with you not here? You know what it'll be like.'

He knew all right. He himself was a little taken aback by her choice, but his own dismay was nothing compared to the brimstone disapprobation that would be his parents' inevitable reaction. Miners were a thriftless, drunken, blasphemous crowd in their eyes and the prospect of a miner—even an ex-miner—marrying their daughter was unthinkable. His boxing and his partiality for a glass of beer would have to be kept quiet for the time being, David realised. He was silent, imagining the meeting of his gentle sister with this robust little man (he remembered having seen him in the boxing-ring as about five-foot-four of bouncy belligerence); the sudden recognition of a mutual attraction; the awareness and eventual admission of love. Megan interpreted his silence as doubtfulness.

'I can't give him up, Dave,' she said shakily. 'I can't. And it's no use my marrying anybody else feeling like this because I know very well if Harry so much as raised his finger I'd go to him no matter who I was married to and no matter what anybody called me.'

She took his breath away with her intensity and he looked at her startled, knowing that he was learning something new about women in general, not just his sister. Taking her by the shoulders he held her away from him and looked steadily into her face.

'Are you quite sure you feel as strongly as that about Harry?' he demanded.

She tried to look shamefaced, but her eyes, staring into his, were shining with emotion as she nodded slowly.

'In that case you'll have to tell Mother and Father and then just dig your feet in,' he said. 'Or I'll tell them, whichever you like. I'd sooner you told Owen yourself, though, I think you ought to do that.'

'Yes, I can now you're here,' she agreed quietly. 'I'll tell them as soon as Father comes home and then I'll go and see Owen.'

They heard their father's voice in the kitchen, and then their mother calling: 'Your tea's ready!' Megan braced herself and they went downstairs.

Their father was already seated at the table, a plate of fish and chips in front of him. His baleful glare switched from David to Megan's defiant expression and his face went as grey as David remembered it when he had thrown the bible at him that night so long ago.

Megan went to her place, but instead of sitting down she gripped the back of her chair and said in a tight voice:

'Dad and Mam. I want to tell you now I'm definitely not going to marry Owen. I don't care if you do call it jilting him but I'm not going through with it, now or ever. David's coming with me tonight and I'm going to cancel all the arrangements.'

The words had squeezed themselves out on one single breath and their father and mother stared at her with the startled concern they might have shown if she had screamed suddenly with pain. Neither of them spoke so Megan drew another breath and continued.

'I'm going to marry Harry Welch. He's the man that did our decorating. I've promised to marry him and it's no good you saying I can't because I'm over twenty-one and you can't stop me from doing it.'

Her mother looked at her father, her eyes urging him to battle, but her father's fierce gaze was still concentrated on Megan as if he wished by its intensity to quell her revolt. Megan weakly flopped down into her chair and bent her head. David saw that his own place had been laid and he too sat down. His mother was already poised on the edge of her chair. Taut with trepidation David and Megan awaited their father's outburst, but with an obvious effort he switched his gaze to his own plate and after a heavy indrawn breath began unfalteringly to intone the grace. David was so startled that he almost missed echoing the 'Amen' but his surprise was tempered with amusement when his father, reaching for the sauce bottle and pouring a pool of it on to the side of his plate, said:

'I'm not going to let any of your sins spoil my tea so you can just keep quiet, all of you, until I've finished.' And taking up his knife and fork he commenced to eat. Mechanically Megan followed his example.

'I didn't buy enough fish for four so you'll have to make do with chips,' David's mother spat at him.

Thank God for that! he thought, and said, 'That's all right.'

The only words spoken during the rest of the meal were when she asked them icily if they were ready for more tea or another slice of bread and butter. Every now and then his father paused, clearing his throat as if he were about to make some pronouncement, but no pronouncement came and eventually he went out to the scullery sink where they heard him coughing up a fish bone. He returned for another cup of tea but as soon as he had drained the last of it he was up out of his chair and into the scullery again. David felt his throat tighten. In the scullery there still hung the strap with which he had chastised them when they were children. Would he dare to intimidate Megan with it now? His sister's eyes were on him, wide with fear. He gave her a reassuring wink, feeling his body tingle with resolution. They heard their father breathing noisily and David relaxed slowly as he realised he was only pulling on the heavy boots he wore when he was going to work on his allotment. His mother realised it too and went out to the scullery; they could hear her whispered remonstrance. What did she want him to do? David wondered.

Then the back door closed and she came back into the kitchen tight lipped and resolute. The relentless interrogation and recriminations began.

What about this Harry Welch? When did he leave the mines? What sort of a home had he? Megan replied in a flat steady tone until her mother uttered scathingly: 'You don't mean to tell me it's that fellow that goes boxing and has his name on the posters outside the public house?'

Megan nodded.

'My daughter mixed up with one of that crowd!' The harsh-voiced denunciation made Megan wince. Her mother braced herself for the question she patently dreaded putting into words.

'Does he drink?'

Megan looked her straight in the face for a moment before her eyes fell. 'Yes, he does like a glass of beer occasionally,' she admitted wanly.

Just for a moment David felt a surge of pity for his mother. It was for her perhaps the bitterest moment of her life. This hitherto submissive daughter of hers was brazenly proposing to unite herself with a man who, in her eyes, was guilty of the worst of all vices! . . . he drank! The quantity did not matter. His crime was that he actually went inside a public house and put a glass of beer to his lips. As a result he was eternally damned.

A derogatory rattle came from her throat—a sound so harsh and offensive that it immediately quelled David's sympathy.

'You'll not be married from this house!' she rapped out and gathering up a pile of dishes from the table she stalked into the scullery. 'That's all I have to say about it.'

Megan's unprecedented rebellion, coming on top of David's delinquency, seemed to have discomfited their parents so thoroughly that in the weeks prior to the wedding they appeared unable to rally their forces against them. Conversation was limited to stiffly uttered question and answer and as a consequence David's desertion of his post at the shop escaped further censure. In the meantime he had sold his motor-cycle so as to buy Megan and Harry a decent wedding present and had been lucky enough to get a temporary job assisting the local surveyor. It was undemanding and monotonous work but he took it with the sole object of earning sufficient money to enable him to buy a few creels so that he could rejoin Donald on the *Silver Spray*, for he had no desire now other than to get back to the sea.

Megan was married without the presence or blessing of her parents in a registrar's office in the nearby town, with David and a boxing crony of Harry's as witnesses and a few friends to boost things along. He saw them off on their honeymoon, Megan glowing with confidence and contentment and Harry all tenderness and pride. David excused himself from the ensuing festivities and hurried home. There was a money order for twenty pounds in his pocket and he wanted to get it off to Donald by the evening's post with a request that he should buy some creels and have them delivered to the *Silver Spray* in readiness for David's arrival the following month. He reckoned by then he should have another twenty as well as enough to keep him going until he started earning.

He supposed it was because he was feeling so pleased with himself when he got back from posting the letter that his parents' glances struck him as being more than usually resentful, but he was too withdrawn to detect anything ominous in their attitudes until after supper when his father cleared his throat several times.

'It's time you made up your mind what you're going to do with yourself, instead of drifting about from job to job,' he challenged.

David had been about to go up to his room and now he paused with his hand on the doorknob.

'I have decided,' he retaliated, a glad conviction sweeping over him as he spoke the words.

'And I've decided too.' His father's voice rose to a bullying shout. 'There's been shame enough brought to this house with my daughter marrying a drunkard. It shall not suffer shame again by harbouring a wastrel.'

'Megan's not married to a drunkard,' David cut in scornfully, but his father silenced him with a gesture that dismissed the subject of Harry.

'I've arranged that your job at the shop is still open for you. They've agreed to overlook your absence and take you on again, but this time there'll be no more fooling around, understand?'

David was aghast at this assumption that he could still be tyrannised over and with anger boiling inside him he said thickly:

'I'm not going back to the shop.'

'What are you going to do?' His mother's interpolation sounded a degree hopeful.

'I'm going fishing up in the north of Scotland,' he told them. 'If you'd asked me I'd have told you that was what I was doing all those weeks I was away. I've been helping a fellow fish lobster creels. It's a good healthy life and I'm planning to go up there and join him again as soon as I've got some money together.'

'Fishing?' his mother echoed incredulously. 'Did you hear that, Dai?'

His father disregarded her. 'I'm telling you once again and once only,' he reiterated. 'Your job is there for you at the shop. Are you going to take it?'

'No. I've decided what I'm going to do with my life and the shop has no part in it.'

His father stood up, resting his hands on the table as if he imagined it to be the pulpit.

'We'll have no fishermen or their kind in this house,' he

declaimed. 'A coarse drunken lot of sinners they are and anyone who goes with them is no son of mine.'

'That's it, then,' David said quietly.

'You mean you'll go back to the shop?' His mother seemed to interpret his words as acquiescence.

'No.' He turned to her. 'I have it all arranged. I'm going next month to start fishing.'

'You'll go now,' commanded his father. 'You'll take your bags and go out of this house and not come back until you've mended your ways.'

David was stupidly hurt; he hadn't wanted the break to be as final as this. Yet now that it had happened he found himself acknowledging its finality.

Upstairs he packed the few things he needed into a rucksack, counted out the money still in his wallet which was just enough to buy his ticket to Scotland and a bar of chocolate for sustenance on the journey. He went downstairs.

His parents were sitting in their chairs on either side of the fireplace as he went through the kitchen to the back door. They did not look up or reply to his goodbye.

Chapter 6

Dawn was only a pale promise through the deck-light on Monday morning when David was shot into wakefulness by the thud of seaboots on the deck. He scrambled out of the bunk and pulling on his clothes threw open the hatch.

'Hallo there!' The salutation was called by a stocky middle-aged man who, from the very briskness of his appearance, David surmised must be one of the relatively few teetotallers among the fishing fraternity of the port. Nimbly and with perfect balance, in spite of the fact that he was carrying a bundle under each arm, he leaped from boat to boat until he reached one of the varnished ringers where he promptly shut himself inside the wheelhouse.

David stood on the fo'c'sle steps and lit his last cigarette. As the light increased very much less brisk figures, their dejectedness recognisable as the afterburden of their weekend orgies, appeared and picked their way across other decks to other boats. They wore the usual denims and thick sweaters, their thigh-boots turned down to flap around their knees.

David was relieved that there was no sign of the crew of the *Fair Lassie*, having planned to justify his presence aboard by having the galley stove lit and the kettle at least showing an intention of coming to the boil in readiness for their arrival. Hurriedly he threw some chunks of wood on the stove, dosed it with paraffin and shut the lid on the resulting gout of flames.

The harbour had a fluttering ceiling of newly aroused gulls; engines were already throbbing; ropes being untied, mooring chains lifted and fenders taken aboard. The crews moved about coiling ropes and tidying decks; taciturn comments were bandied back and forth, while under the covert scrutiny of the skippers of boats tied alongside, those ready for sea were manœuvred out from their berths and their bows brought round to point purposefully towards the harbour entrance. Swiftly and with an increasing urgency of engine noise they got under way, leaving their bow-waves to surge back and set the still moored boats bucking at their ropes with impatience.

The kettle was boiling when there was again a thump on the deck above. Noddy's face appeared in the hatchway.

'How you doin', boy?'

'Fine,' David retorted.

'Rest of the buggers not here yet?' he enquired grumpily.

'Not seen them yet.'

He came down the steps and slumped on a locker, resting his head in his hands. He looked utterly spent, his skin having that arid greyness which a raw peeled potato gets when it has been left for a long time.

'Heavy weekend?' David enquired with flippant sympathy.

Noddy groaned. 'The trouble with me, boy,' he confessed, rubbing his rough hands over his face as if trying to bring it to life, 'when weekends come, I don't just get drunk. I get sodden.'

David grinned. 'Too bad.' He picked up the teapot. 'Like a cup of tea?'

He nodded. 'Aye, but just make me tinker's tea for now. We'll take our tea properly when we get outside a bit way.'

David looked slightly nonplussed and Noddy reached over

for the tea packet, took out a small handful and put it into his mug. 'There now, pour some water on that for me. That's tinker's tea.'

David got out a tin of condensed milk and the canister of sugar and pushed them across the table. He glanced at the thick, dark brew. 'Want a knife and fork for that?' he asked.

'That's the way I like it,' said Noddy.

'That feels better,' he said when he had taken half a dozen hot noisy gulps. 'You found things all right, then?'

'Aye. I fed pretty well, too.' David indicated the boxes. 'There seemed to be plenty there so I tucked in.'

'Just as well you did, boy,' Noddy complimented him. 'Saves the bloody gulls gettin' it.' There were more thumps on the deck.

'That'll be the other two bastards,' he observed mildly. A pair of short thigh-booted legs clumped down the steps followed by Eggo's 'Toorie'-clad head.

Only a couple of seconds later another pair descended, this time succeeded by a sideboard-confined plum-coloured face in which reposed two heavy-lidded eyes of such a grey sadness they seemed to hold the perpetual threat of rain. As Eggo mumbled what was not so much an introduction as a curt explanation of his presence, David was thinking that Brad's flat features were very undistinguished to be those of a reputed lady killer, but then, as Brad thrust out a hand to shake his, his eyelids flicked back with the effect of a suddenly released blind letting in a sparkle that lit his whole face. So that's what the lassies found attractive, David noted.

'All right, let's be away,' said Noddy, rousing himself. His condition seemed in no way to lessen his keenness or his ability to get to sea. Eggo and Brad got into their oilskin smocks and followed him up on deck. Their faces were expressive of acute distaste that might have been for the prospect of work or might just as easily have been because they were smoking the first cigarette of the morning and in their condition it tasted foul. The engine clanged sullenly once or twice, seemed to take heart and settled into a steady throbbing; the ropes came aboard and then the fenders. Without a backward glance from her crew the *Fair Lassie* dipped her way towards the open sea.

Once they had rounded the rugged curve of guano-splashed rocks that held the harbour like a protective arm the light increased with a suddenness that was almost as if a laggard dawn had been given a spirited kick in the pants. The wind too had received a fillip, stirring the sea to restlessness and picking up the bow spray to scatter it along the decks. The propeller was churning the wake into a hissing, tumbling whiteness that sprawled over the water in a pattern of dancing bubbles.

Noddy poked his head out of the wheelhouse.

'Come in here, boy,' he advised. 'It's not so cold as standing out there.' Eggo and Brad were uncovering the hold, releasing the confined smell of the salt bait, so David accepted Noddy's invitation. Elation had wrapped him like an overcoat so that he hadn't realised what an edge the wind had to it until he got inside and shut the door. The wheelhouse was a little cramped with the two of them but it only made for cosiness. There was nowhere to sit; Noddy himself leaned easily against the door, his hands relaxed on the wheel. David wedged himself into a corner.

'Hear all that?' said Noddy.

Above the muted thudding of the engine the shouted morning exchanges between skippers of boats in the vicinity came over the ship-to-ship radio. *Fair Lassie*'s skipper appeared to be indifferent to what was being said but when David asked him how he was liking the look of the weather he replied shortly, 'Good enough, good enough', and as a hint to David to keep quiet he bent his ear attentively towards the radio. Except for a profusion of those epithets with which a fisherman prefaces every noun and without which he appears to be unable to carry on a conversation David found it difficult at first to comprehend what was being said, their diction, now that they were back in the company of the sea, seeming to have become more slurred and scattered with odd vowel sounds and clipped word-endings. After a time, however, his ears began to distinguish some words and after about half an hour they had become thoroughly attuned. He realised that the skippers were recounting their weekend adventures. *Fair Lassie* was eventually hailed and Noddy responded suitably.

'Well, well, and what were you up to yourself at the weekend, you old bugger?' a voice asked and Noddy gave the feeling rejoinder, 'I was my bloody disgusting self, same as usual.' The voice accepted the admission with a throaty sigh that made the radio oscillate.

'You're a bloody fool, man,' another voice condemned.

'Aye, aye,' confirmed Noddy enthusiastically. 'That's what I am, right enough.'

There was a moment's silence and David imagined all the listening men staring out to sea with wide grins transforming their set faces. Then another voice, confessional in its piety, observed:

'We're all bloody fools. Why would we be here where we are, else?' To which sentiment Noddy at least concurred with an equal degree of piety.

The conversation switched to other skippers, other topics, until an urgent voice asking repeatedly for the whereabouts of the *Elizabeth Anne* soared above the rest.

'She's not going out this week,' someone explained at last. 'Her skipper's away to Glasgow to have his arm X-rayed and the boys thought they might just as well take the chance of a few days down there themselves.'

'Lucky sods.' The voice was envious.

'What's wrong with his arm?' a voice demanded with all the petulance of someone who has missed some local titbit of news.

'I don't rightly know. They say he hurt it last time he was beatin' his wife.'

A rumble of sounds came over the air. 'Ach, the man!' David distinguished in a voice that seemed to be edged with humour and then the subject was dismissed as the colourful tales of weekend exploits were resumed.

'My God, but you fellows can swear!' David remarked to Noddy with an admiration that was entirely genuine.

Noddy wiped a grin from his mouth with the back of his hand.

'You can't have to do with the sea and not swear,' he declared solemnly. 'She'd drive you daft if you didn't.'

David waited for him to go on.

'You see, boy, she's not just cruel and savage, but she cheats when you're least expecting her to. She can be that meek and mild one minute and then coming at you in a fury the next. Then perhaps just when you think she's shown you the worst she can do she'll come up with some other dirty trick that can near beat the life out of you and your boat.'

He considered for a moment. 'No, you've got to have plenty of swears to be a match for a bitch like the sea can be. I don't know a fisherman who doesn't swear and I wouldn't believe a man who sails the sea and yet says he never swears. It would be against human nature not to.'

He recollected something. 'I was saying I never knew a fisherman who didn't swear. Well, I'm tellin' a lie then. I did know one who claimed he never swore but like I said he was driven daft by the sea. They found him in bed one weekend with both hands round his throat trying to strangle himself. He never went fishin' again.'

At that moment Brad appeared on deck with the now emptied boxes of stores which he dumped over the side. They stayed on the water attracting the attention of a few gulls until they disappeared slowly from sight. Brad opened the door of the wheelhouse and with a brusque comment took over the helm.

'Come and take your breakfast,' commanded Noddy.

Down in the fo'c'sle the sound radio was emitting the rough-cast wail of a female pop-singer to which Eggo was providing the mellifluous accompaniment of long sucks at his tea mug. In the frying-pan there reposed at least eight fried eggs while inside the oven an enamel dish was piled high with cooked sausages and rashers of bacon. David licked his salty lips at the sight.

'Help yourself,' instructed Noddy, forking four or five rashers and a couple of sausages on to his plate and topping them with two eggs. He was about to add a third egg but changing his mind he slid it back into the pan. 'It's all yours, Brad and Eggo have taken theirs,' he said and sat down, muttering a brief grace. David dug into the bacon and sausages and gloatingly assessing his appetite put three of the eggs on top. Except for the voice of the pop-singer the fo'c'sle went very quiet as they tucked into their piled plates.

'Have another egg,' invited Noddy when he had emptied his plate and David had got through about half of his. 'It'll only go to the gulls if you don't eat it.' There was a shiny trickle of grease down his chin.

'What about you?' David asked, not wishing to be thought as greedy as he felt.

Noddy pushed away his plate and cut himself a thick slice of bread.

'I'm finished except for this,' he admitted. 'I never seem as if I can get an appetite for my breakfast on Monday mornings, same as I can other times.' He used the slice of bread to wipe the grease from his chin, then spread it thickly with butter and spoonfuls of bright red jam from the open tin. David looked enquiringly at Eggo but he too was at the bread-and-jam stage, munching away while all his attention was concentrated on a 'girlie' magazine. David helped himself to more bacon and another egg and by the time he had eaten it he knew he had reached his limit. He leaned back, caressing his stomach contentedly.

'That's the best meal I've had today,' he said.

Eggo looked up and flicked across an opened packet of cigarettes. David took one, saying, 'I think I'll have to give up smoking.'

'Why?' asked Noddy.

'It's getting too expensive.'

'You should smoke a pipe like me,' countered Noddy. 'It doesn't cost near so much.'

Eggo objected. 'I tried it once but I didn't find it worked out any cheaper. You pay just as much for your tobacco after all.'

'Aye, aye,' replied Noddy, cutting off a chunk of thick twist. 'But just you look at this, now. I cut my tobacco and then I rub it out between my hands. Then I fill my pipe, then I light up and in the time it takes me to do all that Beardie here has near finished that cigarette you gave him, you'll see, and he's ready for another.' David glanced down at his nearly finished cigarette and nodded surprised confirmation. 'You smoke a pipe, boy, and you can start enjoyin' it before ever you put a match to it. Not only that, but you've time to think about whether you really need a smoke or not. Gives you time to change your mind like—that's the way it works out cheaper.'

Eggo grunted and returned to his magazine. He flicked over a few pages before thrusting it at David with a salacious smack of his lips.

'Oh boy! Oh boy! Take a look at that now. Doesn't it make you sweat?'

David studied the full-page picture of an alluringly nude female and made responsive noises.

'Ach, Eggo's fairly gone on his naked women,' Noddy

observed contemptuously. He crushed a burned-out match between his fingers and struck another.

David looked up. 'I'm surprised you haven't got a few pin-ups plastered around the place,' he remarked. 'What's a young, handsome crew like yours doing without some juicy nudes to rest their eyes on?'

Eggo shot him an enigmatic glance and snatched back the magazine. Noddy looked at him steadily through the smoke from his pipe. 'You can't go callin' a boat *Fair Lassie* and then stick up pictures of other women all over her,' he reproved patiently. 'She'd be that jealous she'd give you no end of trouble.'

'Aye,' Eggo put in, 'I did try it once but the old cow went right bastardy on us, didn't she, Skipper?'

'She did so,' Noddy agreed. 'The engine broke down twice that week and we had to waste that much time gettin' it sorted we missed a hell of a lot of good fishin'.'

'So the skipper tore down the picture and threw it over the side.' It was Eggo explaining again. 'Right enough we had no more trouble after that.'

David made a mental note of the conversation in case he should ever become a boat owner himself.

'I suppose if she was called some name like the "David Brown" you wouldn't have to worry about little things like pin-ups?' he ventured.

'Ach no,' said Noddy. 'A boat with a name like that wouldn't worry about anythin'.'

Eggo shut the magazine and put it down on the table.

'You just stow that bloody thing under your bunk out of sight,' Noddy cautioned him. With an exasperated epithet Eggo did as he was told.

The radio played a Scottish dance tune. Noddy's eyes brightened and he thumped his fist on the table in time to the music. Eggo's foot was tapping the floorboards. David waited until it had ended before coming out with the question that he had been wanting to ask earlier.

'That fellow they were talking about over the radio. The fellow from the *Elizabeth Anne*, wasn't it? Is he really a wife-beater?' As soon as the words were out of his mouth he felt the question was naive but he was uncertain as yet just how much jesting there was in the conversation of these seemingly dour men.

'Oh, aye, he's that, right enough,' replied Noddy with reluctant enthusiasm.

'She's black and blue more often than not,' confirmed Eggo. 'She's threatened to have the pollis to him more than once but ach, she never does.'

'She's too fond of him, I reckon,' said Noddy.

'Does she deserve it?' David pursued.

'Maybe,' said Noddy.

'I wouldn't think so much of the beatin' of her if he wasn't such a slob himself,' Eggo stormed. 'But he's that bloody lazy it's a wonder he hasn't bought an electric beater to do his dirty work for him.'

David laughed and Noddy let slip an accidental smile.

'I daresay he knows best what suits her.' Noddy betrayed signs of embarrassment. 'An' there's one thing I'll say for him and that is, he's always decent about the way he does it. Now isn't he?' he taxed Eggo.

Eggo concurred lugubriously.

'Decent?' expostulated David. 'What the hell's decent about beating your wife?'

'Well, he always makes sure to see the front door's properly shut before he starts beltin' her so as not to risk upsettin' the passers by,' explained Noddy. 'An' that's decent of him anyway.' He knocked out his pipe on the stove and started to root in his bunk. 'I'll turn in for an hour,' he said. The instant he was in his bunk he was snoring.

Eggo started to collect the soiled dishes.

'I'll wash up,' David offered.

'You can tip that lot over the side first,' Eggo told him, scraping the remaining bacon and sausages into the frying-pan along with the eggs which were still swimming in their inch or so of fat. David took the pan from him.

'What! All this lot?' he exclaimed. 'Won't it warm up for another meal? I wouldn't mind eating it myself later on.'

Eggo's lip twisted so contemptuously that his cigarette teetered and almost fell.

'Throw it out!' he insisted. 'You don't have to look at your food before you eat it on this boat, you know. Those sort of fishin' days are all past, he added meaningly.

'Okay, if that's the way you want it,' said David, but with an anguished expression he popped another sausage into his mouth before he scraped the pan over the side.

Eggo put the mugs and plates into an enamel bowl, shook some detergent over them and poured in boiling water from the kettle. With insensitive fingers he swished the dishes in the water, gave each a cursory wipe with a piece of grey cloth and handed them to David to dry. The tea-towel David had been given was one of two which had come in with the box of groceries. It was shinily new and still bearing its shop creases. When all the dishes had been wiped it was soaking wet and patterned with smears. Eggo took it from him and hung it up to dry above the stove.

'Anything else I can do down here?' David asked when everything had been stowed away.

'Aye,' Eggo said, sweeping the crumbs from the table with the cuff of his jacket. 'You can get the broom and sweep the floor.'

David set to work while Eggo inserted himself into a pair of oilskin trousers and pulled an oilskin smock over his head. As he climbed the steps to the deck he shouted down, 'Got any oilies, Beardie? No? Well, you'll find some in yon bunk,

there. You'll need them if you're comin' up on deck. Aye, an
you'd best stoke the stove before you leave it, but watch yo
do it quietly—if you wake the skipper he'll cuss you all da
for it.'

Chapter 7

Noddy was still snoring when David, clad in his borrowed oilskins, went up to join Brad and Eggo in the wheelhouse. A metal-bright sun had groped its way through the throng of dark clouds that still snarled themselves on the peaks of the mainland hills; it glinted fleetingly on the wings of hovering gulls; it flecked the tossing sea with silver, and threaded the bowspray with segments of rainbows. The chaos of rocks that were the inner islands opened up as *Fair Lassie* approached, revealing a sinuous pattern of tracks that were like raised eyebrows on the face of the moor; their innumerable corries disclosed bright splashes of water. David was assessing the islands for possible climbs which someday he might have the leisure to tackle when Brad spoke.

'I hear you've done a bit of creel settin',' he said.

David told him of his stay on the *Silver Spray* and also of the temporary abandonment of his plan to buy some creels and fish in partnership with Donald.

'Then you'll know a bit about it?' Brad asked. 'About ditchin' crabs and things and re-baitin' so that you can give us a hand?'

'Aye, and he'll know about Hairy Wullies,' put in Eggo.

David shook his head.

'You don't? Ach, you wait until you come across them

78

buggers dodgin' all over the deck without you ever seein' them move. An' the way they look at you too, as if they're tryin' to hypnotise you.' Eggo hunched his fat shoulders in an attempt to shudder. 'They fairly give you the creeps.'

'Hairy Wullies?' David repeated wonderingly. He suspected that they were perhaps the equivalent of the 'gremlins' known to air crews. 'What do they look like?'

'Oh, just horrible black hairy buggers,' said Eggo, going out of the wheelhouse and slamming the door behind him.

'You know somethin', Beardie,' Brad began and then paused to lean over and tug at the strap of the already tightly closed wheelhouse window. 'Yon fishin' that Donald does is not the way to make a bit of money,' he continued. 'It's too titchy a way altogether except for a man that has a wife to keep him like he has. What you want to try for is a job on a bigger boat that's fishin' say a couple of hundred creels or more.' He tipped the ash from his cigarette into the handy top of his thigh-boot. 'Mind you,' he went on, 'the herrin's where the big money lies these days.'

'I wonder you're not trying for the herring yourself, then,' David said.

'I'll be doin' that,' Brad assured him. 'Just as soon as Noddy's ready to pack up with the lobsters I'm away to claim my berth on a ringer. I had it last year and I'm promised it again for the winter.'

'It's tougher, isn't it?' David asked.

'Oh, aye, it's tough but a man can be well on the way to ownin' his own boat after a few years stint at the herrin'. With a bit of luck and under the "Grant and Loan" scheme, of course,' he added.

David asked if Eggo had similar plans.

'Ach, I believe he's happy just as he is, fishin' creels,' Brad replied. 'I think he'd like to get his own boat right enough some time, it's only natural, but Eggo's in no hurry. He's not so keen on the herrin' for a start. He fairly likes his sleep, does Eggo, and you don't get much chance of sleep when you're fishin' herrin'.' He broke off, excitedly calling David's attention to a bobbing raft of a hundred or so shags inshore of the boat. 'Now, if I had my gun with me I could take a pot at that lot. I once got seven of the buggers with one shot and we had skart for our dinners for a week.' Ruefully his gaze followed the 'skarts'. Involuntarily it seemed his hands on the wheel headed the boat towards them. The birds twisted their necks apprehensively and tensed themselves for flight. With a regretful sigh Brad turned the bow back to their original course. At the same time he returned to the subject of Eggo.

'You'd never think Eggo had been a brilliant scholar from the way he is now, would you?'

'No,' admitted David with surprise. 'He's sharp, I noticed that, but I shouldn't have thought he was all that brilliant.'

'Well then, it's true. Dux of the school every year, he was. His father sent him to one of these swanky boardin' schools too with the intention of makin' him a professor or somethin'. His father was never at the sea, of course—he was one of these puly-wally "Come to Jesus" fellows, if you know what I mean?'

David nodded comprehension.

'His grandfather was at the fishin', though,' Brad resumed, 'and he couldn't have done so badly at it either for when he died he left Eggo's father a good lump of money. Anyway, they say that's what paid for Eggo to go to a swanky school. He did well too, passed all his exams and learned to speak with strings of long words that nobody here had as much as heard of. His father was fairly chuffed with him. But when Eggo left school he took to hangin' round the boats, just like the rest of the lads here. He'd get out for a trip first with one and then with another until he landed this berth with Noddy and he's stayed with him ever since. Just a plain bloody fisherman like the rest of us, Eggo is now, an' speakin' the same language. His old man wouldn't talk to him for a long time after he'd taken to the fishin' but ach, I think he realised at last the sea had beaten him. Now he contents himself with singin' hymns about the perils of the sea and just puts on his coat and rushes out of the house when Eggo's swearin' gets too much for him.'

'Aye?' said David quizzically.

'True as I'm here,' affirmed Brad. 'An' the only times you'll ever hear Eggo use a long word now is when he's drunk. He talks like a walkin' dictionary then, but as for bein' a professor, well, all he uses his brains for now is thinkin' up new threats and curses to use. He can fairly do that sort of thing.' Brad's voice took on a reverential tone. 'I daresay you've heard a sample or two already?' He cocked an eyebrow at David and was answered by a smile. 'Aye, but there's a good laugh in it when Eggo gets into a bit of a tear and comes out with somethin' he's thought up.' He gave a dry chuckle. 'Not that Eggo ever gets proper ratty. He just likes to make himself sound savage and he always waits to get everybody quiet before he comes out with his curse. He'd make a right good comedian would Eggo.'

The boat speared on, leaving islands behind and yet still pointing her way to more distant islands that were as yet only glimpsed peaks peering above a rumpled sea. Noddy, looking a different man after his brief rest, came up from the fo'c'sle, went to the stern and relieved himself before taking over the wheel while Brad went below to put on his oilskins. The engine slowed a pace as they came into the lee of a small island that looked as if it might have been doodled on to the sea much as a child doodles syrup from a spoon on to its plate.

'Okay, there she is!' shouted Noddy as they sighted an orange buoy, its cheek against the water. Noddy gently eased the boat forward. Both Brad and Eggo were on deck now, waiting; Eggo holding the boathook in readiness as the buoy bobbed towards the starboard bow. He bent forward and with a deft twist of the boathook caught the rope of the buoy and lifted it aboard.

'Okay!' shouted Noddy again. His eyes were aware, watchful for every condition of tide, drift and direction but his expression remained reflective. The engine was throttled right down now to no more than a religious murmur and suddenly it seemed to David that there had been no cessation of noise but rather that a great silence had been broken as all the sounds of the sea closed in on them. There came the surging hiss of swell on the beach; its slapping and patting at the rocks; its teasing chuckles and appreciative gurgles round the boat. A panic of oystercatchers rose, wheeled and with a medley of shrieking and a hurry of soft wing-beats flew overhead. From ashore the sound of a waterfall came to them as a whisper.

Brad ran to the winch and the rope came in slowly, water peeling off it on to the deck. At the gunwale Eggo waited for the first creel to surface. David watched the competent rhythm of their movements: Brad flicking the rope off the winch and back again as a creel came up; Eggo bending to swing it aboard, unlacing it, reaching out the lobster—when there was a lobster, hurling away unwanted crabs, re-baiting and lacing it and stacking it in position before moving back to the gunwale ready for the next.

'Right now, boy,' Noddy said, 'I daresay you could give them a hand. Just see and look out for holes in the net.'

Eagerly David went to join them, to become himself caught up in the unconscious ballet of their routine. He took his place beside Eggo, exulting that he knew what to do without instruction. Not that either of the men would at this crucial stage have wasted time on explanations; an epithet and a rough push to get him out of the way would have been their only comment on his inadequacy. Eggo hoisted a creel on to the gunwale amid a swilling of water that poured down the front of his smock; there was a tumbling of small sea creatures and weed from the net; the clacking of a lobster's tail. He pushed the creel towards David and immediately David's fingers flew to unlace the netting door at the top. His quick, wary hand picked out the lobster and threw it into one of the boxes on the deck. Deftly he gathered up the stale bait and the sea debris that had collected in the creel and flung it back into the water: the spider's parlour was clean and tidied. Quickly he jammed new bait into the string loop and slid the knot down firmly: now the table was laid. He made a quick check for tears in the netting through which a lobster might escape and laced up the door. He put the creel with the rest in time to take the next one.

At the end of the fleet the second buoy came aboard, and David staggered back against the roar and thrust of the engine as the boat shot forward. He leaned back on the stacked creels watching the land spinning by and realised as his clothes pressed cold against his back how much he must have been sweating. The engine slowed again as the boat slid in even closer to a rock-studded bay where seabirds bobbed on the lifting swell and fished and quarrelled domestically. Above the entrance to a deep cave a ragged line of 'skarts' stood holding out their wings to dry in the pale sunshine in much the same attitude as a woman holds out her newly varnished fingernails. Below the cave on a chunky rock David discerned the sleek shape of a seal hauled out for a siesta. Its bright eyes watched the *Fair Lassie*'s approach with mounting alarm and he saw it squirming uneasily in its blubber before it struggled clumsily and slid with a 'plop' into the sea. Some distance from their stern its head bobbed up again and David grinned as he saw it regarding the boat with renewed nose-in-the-air confidence.

A shout from Noddy came as the engine sank once again

into its quiet murmur. With a lilting sweep of body and arms Brad threw over the buoy and the wet black rope snaked out after it. Eggo held the first creel, which had been the last one to come aboard, poised on the gunwale.

'That's it,' said Noddy and Eggo pushed the creel over the side while Brad let the rope pay out smoothly from its neat coil on the deck. David watched the rope keenly. The docility with which it was running through Brad's hands was deceptive and a kink or a catch through a too slow reaction would have turned it into a demon without mercy. At the exact moment of tightening Eggo let the second creel go, the tumbled water received it, accepted it and let it sink slowly out of sight. The rest of the fleet followed and without respite they were off again in search of the next and the next as the hauling and re-setting continued.

'You can go and peel some spuds now!' David heard Eggo's shouted instruction as they were working towards the last buoy of the last fleet. 'An' cut 'em up chip-size while you're at it,' he added. David was astonished when he got to the fo'c'sle to see that the clock said it was already four. 'Put the kettle on and pull that damper out of the stove.' Eggo's voice came down the hatchway as the boat was turned towards her night anchorage. Minutes later Eggo thumped down the steps, rooted in the butcher's box, extracted half a dozen succulent-looking chops and rammed them into a roasting tin. After smothering them with dripping he pushed them into the oven and darted quickly back to the deck. David heard the noise of boxes being dragged about as the lobsters were packed into them and the lids nailed securely. By the time Eggo reappeared David already had the potatoes chipped and a pan of fat melting on the stove.

'Shall I pop some of these in now?' he asked Eggo.

Eggo, busy at the contents of the stores locker, glanced over his shoulder at the pan.

'No, you ignorant slob. Can't you see the fat's not hot enough yet?'

David looked puzzled. 'How am I going to know that?' he demanded.

'Spit in it, of course,' responded Eggo testily.

'Spit in it?' David looked askance at Eggo's back.

'Aye.' Eggo turned irritably with an oath for David's stupidity. 'Did you never see your mother spit on her iron to see was it hot enough? Well, then. Do the same with the chip fat. When it's hot enough it'll spit back at you.' He demonstrated and the fat retorted with a reticent sizzle. 'See?' he said and turned back to the cupboard. After a few minutes he spat into the pan again, dodging the retaliatory eruption with the skill of long practice. 'Okay, now,' he confirmed. 'Time to shove 'em in.'

Fair Lassie had by this time reached quiet water. The anchor had been dropped and the engine silenced. Eggo stayed to finish the cooking while David went up to clear the deck of its involuntary stowaways, the little scuttling crabs, starfish, shells, weed and tiny fish. He gathered them up, seeing the patterns and colours of the seabed slithering in his fingers and aware of quick nips from small anxious lives he tossed them back home and swilled the deck.

Noddy, Brad and Eggo had already drunk one pot full of tea by the time he returned to the fo'c'sle. 'We was fairly parchin' for it,' Noddy explained. Eggo ladled out plates of thick brown soup and when they had finished that the chops and chips were ready. Gasping and blowing at the heat of them they tucked in. Already, after taking only two meals aboard, David had come to appreciate the need for those prodigious parcels of food that had, so short a time ago, astonished him. Appetites at sea were voracious and this combined with the speed with which meals were habitually consumed meant that the cook must always err on the side of prodigality. High food bills for the boat would never be a cause for recrimination but not to have plenty of food already cooked so that second and third helpings were not to hand if needed would have resulted in the cook finding himself without a berth.

When they had disposed of all the chops and chips they wiped their plates clean with slices of bread. Eggo opened a tin of fruit and a tin of milk and they filled up any emptiness they may still have felt with bread and jam washed down by more tea.

The radio was on but they talked above it. The day's haul, David gathered, had been a satisfactory one with the lobsters coming at a good average weight. Large lobsters, he was told, rarely bring the highest prices. The crew were optimistic about the prospects for the rest of the week. Noddy, quoting the ship-to-ship radio, regaled them with details of the catches of other boats and with anecdotes from the conversations he had overheard while in the wheelhouse. He became contemplative and David thought he must be listening for some sound of wind or tide but with startling suddenness he jumped up. His fingers were already pulling at his trouser belt as he disappeared into the hold. Later there came the sound of a bucket being emptied over the side and dipped several times to sluice it clean. The *Fair Lassie*, David had discovered, offered no such refinement as a w.c. as did the more up-to-date boats. A battered galvanised bucket with a rope tied to its handle was the uncomfortable substitute so that cacation was a martyrdom. David knew that if he was to be a fisherman he must discipline his bowels as he must discipline his stomach and his need for sleep to accept the erratic.

Noddy, looking much refreshed, returned to the fo'c'sle and Brad looking resolute went into the hold. David wondered if there was a strict order of precedence and decided he must wait until Eggo had taken his turn. Suddenly David remembered that he had completely forgotten to wash out his dog-soiled trousers the previous day as he had intended, and the memory caused him to exclaim aloud. Eggo and Noddy stared at him expectantly and David related the incident of the dog. Noddy's eyes lit with merriment and Brad coming back in time to hear the end of the story abandoned himself to laughter. Eggo hid his own amusement and turned on David with simulated rage.

'You mean to say you've been sittin' in the same place as me and eatin' your food at the same table and you with your trousers pickled in dog's piss? God! It's enough to turn a man's stomach. Get you up there and wash 'em quick or what you'll get for your breakfast tomorrow is sausages and soup in a po.'

Brad humphed. 'That the best you can do, Eggo?' he asked contemptuously. 'I could have thought of as good as that myself.'

'It's good enough for now,' returned Eggo with a trace of hurt pride. 'It's a sight that's made plenty of strong men fetch up before now I can tell you.'

'That would have been Bessie's dog, likely?' interrupted Noddy, his face still touched with the afterglow of his smile. 'A great black dog, would it be? A labrador, I think she calls it?'

'Aye, that would be it,' David agreed. 'It was Bessie who was with it at the time, anyway.'

'Oh, him!' said Brad, claiming David's attention. 'Well now, Beardie, I'll tell you a tale about that dog. It's not the first time it's lifted its leg on a decent man, and it happened this way. Bessie had it on a long chain when she took it down to the pier one day. Big Cam was there watchin' the boats unload. He had his seaboots turned down round his knees as usual and he was standin' with one leg on the rail not payin' any particular attention when up walks this dog to him and pisses right down inside Big Cam's boot. Bessie just stood

87

there, holdin' on to the chain and gapin' till Big Cam, feelin' what's happened to him, turns round to her and says, "Your dog's had his piss now, Bessie, don't you think it's time you should pull the chain?" '

Eggo got out the washing-up bowl. Just as it had after breakfast the fat from the frying-pan went over the side along with the chop bones and tea slops. 'An' don't tell me we should keep the fat,' Eggo warned. 'I tried once puttin' it in a tin to keep it but we got a bit of a pastin' before it had time to set and the whole bloody lot fell out of the cupboard and spilled over the floor.'

'By God, no, chum, don't try that again,' exhorted Brad. 'The fo'c'sle here was worse than a skatin' rink and we took it on deck on our boots. It took us weeks to get rid of it properly and it was a miracle one of us didn't go over the side before we did.'

When the dishes had been washed and more stains added to the tea-towel they slumped in their seats. Noddy and David went through the Sunday papers. Brad took out a hard-backed book of football pictures—he was a fervent Celtic supporter. Eggo produced a mouth-organ and began trying over some pop tunes, competing with a military band on the radio. He began to play a traditional Scottish melody and immediately Noddy, reaching up a hand, turned down the radio, so that it was just audible enough to catch his attention if there was a gale warning. Eggo was a skilful performer and they hummed the tunes and tapped their feet to the rhythms between reading and commenting about murders and marriages, perverts and politics and all the shoddinesses of urban life. Noddy threw his own paper down in disgust.

'I feel sorry for the men that has to work these printing machines,' he said, 'being forced to read every word of that muck.'

Brad gave himself up to a loud and luxurious yawn. 'I'm

for crashing it,' he said and climbed into his bunk. Eggo put down his mouth-organ and taking up the long iron poker started to rattle away at the stove. Finally he drove the poker deep into the ashes and levered them up to let some air in. Leaving it like that he resumed his mouth-organ.

With the avowed intention of dipping his trousers over the side before nipping quickly into his bunk, David went on deck, but once there the enchantment of the night held him captive. After the sleep-inducing fugginess down below the chill breeze smacked at his salt-burned face like a gentle reproof. As his eyes accustomed themselves to the darkness he could see that the boat was lying in a stretch of placid water sheltered by two craggy horns of land which butted out into the sea and converged towards a narrow passage which looked just about wide enough for the full beam of the boat with perhaps a foot or so to spare either side. The crowded rocks looked velvet black against a sky that was sown with stars so bright that their reflections danced in the lazy ripples around the boat. The breeze was humming in the rigging, making a fitful harmony with the strains of 'My Ain Folk' which were coming through the hatchway. Coquettish little waves teased at the shore.

The chill of the night began to prick through his clothes. He slipped off his trousers and dunked them several times over the side before hanging them over the mast to dry. Shivering he made a dash for the fo'c'sle. Eggo was pulling the red-hot poker from the stove.

'Did you wash out those pants of yours?' Eggo demanded aggressively.

'Can't you see I did?' David snapped through chattering teeth.

Eggo held up the poker menacingly. 'It's a damn' good job for you that you did. If you hadn't I was goin' to ram this poker up your arse-hole,' he threatened. 'Aye,' he added with great relish, 'I'd have rammed it up handle end first too, so that you'd have burned your hands pullin' it out.'

David insinuated himself into his bunk and gave one chuckle before he was asleep.

Chapter 8

They were back in the same anchorage the following two nights, the catches of lobsters being good enough to necessitate their moving the creels only a little further each day instead of having to ferry them, two or three fleets at a time, to completely new fishing grounds.

'It's a real Bobby's job we've got this week,' Eggo declared. 'Nothin' to do but keep an eye on things and then help yourself to the loot.' The evening meal was over and they were enjoying their customary laze in the fo'c'sle.

'Aye, aye, Beardie'll learn what hard work is like when we run into a bit of bad weather and after all the slog of liftin' the creels come in with no beasties in them,' Eggo said.

'Aye,' agreed Brad. 'If you're goin' to haul for nothin' I'd sooner do it in fine weather.'

'There's no creel so heavy as a creel with no lobster in it,' expounded Eggo.

'Ach, hard work was never easy.' Noddy's final comment was delivered as he tucked himself into his bunk and prepared for instant sleep by closing his eyes and letting his mouth fall open.

Brad stood up and stretched as far as he could in the small amount of headroom. 'Oh, well, I suppose I'd best turn in too. The more sleep I get the more fit I'll be for Saturday.'

'Anything doing on Saturday besides wenching and drinking?' David asked sceptically.

'There's a dance,' said Eggo. 'Would you like me to get you a couple of lassies to go with?'

'If he stays sober all the lassies will be beggin' for him,' put in Brad. 'That's all some 'em go for. I think they enjoy dancin' better than anythin' else.' His voice was touched with sleepy incredulity.

'Do you go to the dance?' David asked him.

'I go, but not to dance.' Brad got into his bunk and pulled the blanket up over his face.

David turned to Eggo. 'What about you? Are you a dancer?'

'Not me,' Eggo denied. 'Mind you, I'd dance if I could,' he went on earnestly, 'but I can't somehow seem to learn to dance.'

'What do you do with yourself on Saturdays, then?' David pursued.

'Oh, I go to the dance all right,' Eggo replied. 'But I get drunk first and then I don't notice whether or not I'm dancin'. It passes the time,' he added sadly. He too prepared to turn in. David put a foot on the first of the steps and Eggo chaffed, 'What the hell are you goin' up there for at this time of night? Is there somethin' wrong with your insides that you can't keep it till mornin'?' David laughed and climbed up through the hatchway.

These few minutes alone on deck before he sought his bunk were his only privacy. He liked to lean against the mast listening to the sounds of the night and meditating on the lessons in seamanship, natural history and fishing skills and profanity he had learned during the day. He liked to look forward to increasing his knowledge of all four subjects on subsequent days. He was about to go below when the spotlight of a boat appeared in the passage way between the rocks. Because he had heard no engine noise David was momentarily startled, even suspicious. Was it poachers? Silent, except for the hiss of a bow-wave, she came in and alongside. David knew a moment's panic as he caught sight of the grotesque faces of the men standing on her deck. His mind leaped to legends of phantom ships and ghostly raiders.

'Eggo,' he called down the hatch. 'For Christ's sake come and look at this.'

'Go to hell, you silly slob,' retorted Eggo truculently and when David looked up again the grotesque faces had been replaced by those of men he half recognised as having seen in the pub the previous Saturday. He was ashamed of his momentary fear.

'Are your fenders out?' a voice that was like the tearing of thick fabric instructed rather than asked a question. 'We'll tie up alongside you for the night.'

'Aye, okay,' David called, and caught the rope they flung to him. 'Who are you?' he asked, as he made fast the rope.

'*Fragrant Air*', returned a gruff voice.

The two boats swung companionably together. The crew started to take off their oilskins and the skipper, coming out of the wheelhouse, stepped aboard *Fair Lassie*.

'Where's Noddy?' he demanded.

'In his bunk,' David told him. 'And the other two.'

'I'll soon have the buggers out of it,' he promised cheerfully and went down below.

David went aboard the other boat. 'Will somebody tell me what the hell you were wearing on your faces when you came in just now?' he challenged them.

The men laughed. 'Yogi Bear masks,' they explained. 'We've been havin' a lot of trouble with them bloody scalders. The creels and ropes were comin' up covered with the things and they were stingin' our hands and faces till we had to leave one fleet altogether. The skipper had to go ashore to telephone and he happened to see these false faces in the Post Office shop, so he bought half a dozen of them. They're grand

93

for the job. We went back and lifted the fleet we'd left. In fact we've only just finished cleaning the stings from the ropes and from the deck. That's why we were still wearin' them when we came in.'

One of the men picked up a mask and handed it to David. 'You should get yourself one next time you're in port,' he told him. 'They're the best answer we've found yet to the scalders. I can put up with them stingin' my hands but when they get on my face it's a different story altogether.'

'You gave me a bit of a turn when I first saw you,' David admitted.

'Aye, I can believe that,' the man agreed.

From below came the smell of roasting meat accompanied by a peremptory summons from the cook. 'See you later,' the men called as their heads bobbed down the hatch.

Aboard the *Fair Lassie* the skipper of the *Fragrant Air*, a rotund little man whose tight trousers were filled to bursting point by his fat round behind, had got Noddy out of his bunk and was urging him to 'Come and have a wee crack with us'. Noddy was soon persuaded and David was also pressed into going along. Eggo and Brad only swore profusely when they were approached. Eggo was still swearing in his sleep when David carefully closed the hatch behind them.

The crew of the other boat had already finished their meal and they moved along to make room for Noddy and David on the lockers. The skipper, ignoring the full plate of soup awaiting him on the stove, produced a bottle of whisky from a locker. The cook produced some glasses—David suspected they came from under his mattress—and set one in front of each man. That fishing boats should carry, among the rough comforts of their fo'c'sles, such fragile things as whisky glasses had caused David some surprise but once he had come to realise how much a Scotsman reveres his native drink his only surprise was that they were content with such glasses as they had.

The bottle was emptied and the skipper produced another, though he ate his soup before opening it. The cook brewed up in a teapot that held about eight pints, and they drank tea laced with whisky.

'You were awful late in,' Noddy observed after a while. 'Did somethin' keep you back?'

The *Fragrant Air* was a bigger boat than the *Fair Lassie* and fished many more creels but it was unusual for any lobster boat not to have reached her night's anchorage until so long after darkness had fallen. The inference would be that she had been doing some illicit fishing.

'Did you no' hear me sayin' over the radio the reason for it?' asked the skipper.

'I did not,' replied Noddy with sudden interest. 'What was all that, then?'

'We found a body!' announced the skipper.

'You did?' echoed Noddy, his eyes flicking wide

'Aye we did so. I reckon it must have been one from that boat that was lost a week or so back. It fairly looked as though it had been a while in the water anyway.'

'Oh, here, here,' said Noddy with infinite compassion.

'Aye, the poor bastard.' The touching comment came from a man on David's right.

'You didn't take it in tow, surely?' Noddy enquired.

'Nah, nah.' There was distaste in the skipper's tone. 'No, what we did was that I went ashore where there was a Post Office and made a call to the police. I told them where it was and where it would likely be by this evening so it's their job to see to it now.'

'Aye.' Noddy pondered a moment and then in a voice that sounded slightly strained he asked, 'Did you have a wee bitty earth for it?'

'Oh, surely we did,' answered the skipper promptly to the accompaniment of murmured corroboration from his crew.

David asked: 'Why earth?'

Noddy exchanged a glance with the skipper before beginning to explain. 'Well, Beardie, there's a belief among us fishermen that if you find a body in the sea and you don't scatter a bit of earth on it, the next corpse that will be found will be your own.'

Already acquaintance with the sea had taught David that all fishermen are intensely superstitious. From his own experience he knew that no matter how downright and practical a person you might be ashore, once you started to earn your living from the sea you must recognise her witchery and accept that she must be placated by crossed fingers or touched wood or by some such gesture for every rash act committed or every rash word spoken. Even so, Noddy's explanation still left him puzzled.

'Where and how,' he ventured to ask, 'when you're at sea do you manage to find earth on a fishing boat?'

'Well, we found enough at the bottom of the potato sack.' The cook supplied the information. 'We wouldn't have had any otherwise, except maybe a bit of sand or coal dust from the bilges.'

'I wonder if that would have done?' asked a serious voice.

'I wouldn't want to risk it,' said Noddy. 'I always carry a pail of earth myself. It's handy anyway in case you get a bit of a fire on board.'

'What about these small boats that go out fishing from the islands and come back each evening? They don't carry coal or potatoes with them and surely they don't clutter up what space they have with a bucket of earth just because some day they might come across a floating corpse?'

'They wouldn't need to take a bucket,' Noddy told him with great patience. 'But those boats always carry a sod with them anyway.'

'A sod? What for?'

Noddy gave him a lenient smile. 'To cac on,' he explained. 'These islemen find it more natural for them than a bucket.'

'Ach, to hell with corpses,' said the skipper. 'Let's have a game of cribbage. Anybody playin'?'

It was the cook who produced a pack of cards and also what looked like a bible, and once again David suspected they were from under his mattress. When he had placed the pack on the table the cook disappeared with the bible through the doorway into the hold. Returning after a minute or two he climbed straightaway into his bunk.

'Isn't he playing?' David asked.

'Not him.' The skipper drew in a reproving breath. 'Tolly doesn't hold with gamblin', do you, Tolly?' There was no answer from the bunk.

'And yet what's fishin' but gamblin'?' the man on David's right demanded. 'You stake your boat and your gear and your lives against the sea and it's only luck whether or not you get anythin' comin' up.'

'That's true,' opined Noddy.

'Aye, right enough,' the skipper agreed. 'But you know old Tolly. Comes aboard every Monday mornin' with a bible in one hand and a bottle of whisky in the other and it's a dram and a text every night before he turns in. He's a good cook though, is Tolly, and a good fisherman too, I'll say that for him.'

'Aye, and he's a good mate,' enthused the man on David's right.

'None better,' corroborated the man opposite.

A long snore of acquiescence came from the cook's bunk and the men turned their attention to the cards.

David threw in his hand after he had been playing for an hour and went to his bunk. Noddy looked as if he had every intention of playing cribbage all night. Next morning, an hour before their own alarm clock shrilled its testy summons, David was awakened by the noise of the *Fragrant Air*'s engines as they got under way. Simultaneously there was some irritable chaffing from Noddy.

'Come on, let's be off, you lazy buggers. Thinkin' of stayin' in your bunks all day, are you?'

'What the hell!' demanded Brad aggressively.

'Let a man have his sleep, you old bodach,' Eggo grumbled, flopping out of his bunk like something it had regurgitated.

'You young fellows'll never make fishermen,' declared Noddy, pulling on his boots. 'You're too damn' soft. Wantin' to lie in your bunks while there's light to fish and always hastin' to get back to port for the weekend. Aye, and wantin' to lay the boat up while you take a holiday every year.'

'A man needs his sleep and he needs his weekends if he's to work properly for the rest of the time,' Brad told him grumpily.

'Aye, and he needs a holiday, the same as other people,' said Eggo. He pulled a second thick pullover over his head.

'It's no way to make money,' insisted Noddy. 'Look at the skipper of the *Flame* now,' he continued. 'He was a damn' good fisherman. He didn't take weekends off nor holidays or anythin' else and look at the money he left behind when he died.'

'Aye, and how old was he when he died?' Brad asked meaningly.

'Forty,' declared Noddy. 'No more than forty and by that time he'd made forty thousand pounds. Forty thousand!' he repeated and the reverence in his tone was unmistakable.

'And what's the good of forty thousand pounds to him now, tell me that?' Brad's voice was scornful.

'I'd sooner not work so hard and live a bit longer even if I left nothin',' said Eggo.

'What? And have it put in the papers that you'd not made enough money to leave some behind?' Noddy expostulated. 'People would say that you were either a bloody fool or a bad fisherman.'

'I couldn't care less what they say about me when I'm gone,' Eggo said defiantly. 'I'll not be hearin' it.'

'Maybe so. Maybe so,' conceded Noddy. 'But for myself I wouldn't like it said I wasn't a good fisherman.'

Unwashed and unkempt David and Brad went to lift the anchor. The morning seemed only half awake as the boat nosed between the rocks and out into the sleepy grey sea. The hills were powdered with hoar frost and as they passed close beneath their craggy shoulders David caught sight of a stag leading five hinds along a precipitous path. The stag paused, turning its antlered head to watch the progress of the boat, no doubt assessing her menace. Reassured he went purposefully on, the hinds following with faltering, early morning reluctance, as if protesting that they had not yet had time to rub the sleep from their eyes.

The first fleet of creels was hauled but as the second fleet came up Eggo broke into a stream of vituperation. 'Them bloody scalders!' he screamed. David looked down at the creel just emerging from the water and saw it festooned with the long tendrils of stinging jellyfish. He joined in Eggo's invective as the slimy stingers wrapped themselves round his hands and splashed up into his face. His beard protected him to some extent but when a rope flicked accidentally across his eyes he found too late that he had rubbed in the stinging slime. The pain was excruciating and he stumbled to the wheelhouse, fearing that he had damaged his sight irreparably.

'Quick! Go and dip your face in fresh water,' Noddy instructed. David crawled along the deck to the fo'c'sle.

The fresh water brought a degree of immediate relief and it was not long before he was able to resume his work on the deck. Though his eyelids felt as if they had been dipped in quicklime his sight, he was relieved to find, was unaffected. The hauling and the setting and the malediction continued.

Noddy decided to move all the creels that day to new ground and they laid them around the shores of a craggy, shingle-fringed island which boasted a half-dozen or so small houses dotted about a few acres of wind-sleeked moor.

'I might have stayed there the night but the forecast's that the wind's goin' round to the west,' said Noddy. 'If it does it'll blow straight in there and it's no place for a boat to be.' He brought the boat round, as if still undecided whether to go or stay. 'I know a fellow that lives up here,' he went on, 'and if he'd seen us he would have come out in his boat and taken us ashore for a ceilidh.'

Getting ashore from the *Fair Lassie* unless there happened to be a convenient pier was practically impossible. They carried no boat—not even a raft or a rubber dinghy—every inch of space being required, so the crew maintained, for the equipment necessary for fishing creels. Already David had experienced a sense of frustration when, anchored in the shelter of the small, inviting looking bay, he had found there was no way of getting ashore for an hour's exploration, short of peeling off his clothes and swimming for it. He had to be honest with himself and admit he wasn't much of a swimmer.

'What the hell are we muckin' about at?' Eggo's voice demanded irascibly and Noddy, recollecting himself, turned the boat's stern to the shore and allowed her to cleave her way through the ruffled sea towards a quieter anchorage.

'This fellow I was after tellin' you about,' resumed Noddy who, with work finished, tended to become reminiscent. 'When he was a boy there was only his own house that was inhabited on that island. All the rest was in ruins where folks had given up and gone away. Hector, that was his name, lived there with his mother and his sister. I don't mind that he ever had a father, not to speak of, anyway. His mother was a fine woman I believe and she kept a cow and some hens and a few sheep and it was herself used to go out and catch fish for them and grow the potatoes. She spun and wove the tweed too and perhaps three or four times every year she'd row over to one of the bigger islands where she could send away her weavin' to some place that would buy it from her. She'd never take the boy with her and so from the time he was born he never saw another human being in his life but his mother and sister. Mind that, now,' Noddy repeated, glancing at David to make sure he was sufficiently impressed. 'Nine years old, he was, before he saw another soul.' Assured of David's attention he went on: 'He told me himself he was out on the moors one day when he saw a man comin' towards him. Never havin' seen a man before he thought it must be some strange beast and he was that scared he ran all the way home and hid himself in the loft. The man came to the house and the mother took him in and gave him a cup of tea and there all the time was wee Hector up in the loft peepin' down at him and wonderin' whatever was happenin'. His mother was that vexed with herself that she took him with her after that when she went to sell her tweed but Hector said it was two years or more before he could get used to people enough to speak to them.'

'It doesn't seem possible,' objected David.

'It's what he told me himself,' averred Noddy. 'Aye, and I believe it right enough. It was durin' the war, you see, and there wasn't the visitors to these islands that you get now.'

'Did you say he's still living there?' David asked.

'Aye, he's still there. He joined up in the last war and was put into the Navy. He went all over the world then but when it was over he just came back here and settled down. Now a stranger talkin' to him would never know but that he'd ever left the island.'

'Didn't he marry?'

'Aye, he married and had a son that was in the Merchant Navy. He got drowned a while back.'

'If you're talkin' about old Hector I can tell you he had a couple of daughters too.' Brad had just joined them in the wheelhouse. 'Nice girls they are, too.'

'Aye, that's right, so he did,' Noddy recalled. 'One of

them's married to a banker in America and the other one's a nurse in a big hospital in London. She's doin' well at it too.'

'She's at home again now,' Brad corrected him. 'She's stayin' to look after her parents.'

'Is that so? Aye well, I daresay it makes a change for her,' Noddy observed.

It was getting dark now but just before it had set the sun had appeared briefly from behind a phalanx of black cloud to spread the horizon with a peculiar yellow light.

'I don't like the look of that,' said Noddy. He turned to David. 'That's what some folks in these parts call the "mariners' storm lanterns".'

Brad and David paid little heed to his remark. They had had a long and heavy day and were at the stage of tiredness which Eggo had defined as 'If I take a deep breath I'll be asleep'. They had come within sight of the cove that was to be their anchorage for the night and could think only of the prospect of full bellies to be followed by the snug embrace of their bunks. Suddenly the *Fair Lassie* juddered, her engine raced, paused and roared again. The propeller thrashed as Noddy went full astern. There was a moment of voiceless panic before Brad and David burst out of the wheelhouse. The water had ceased to fall away from the bows. Brad grabbed the long boathook and kneeling in the bows began prodding at the water. Eggo's horrified face appeared out of the hatchway.

'Shift them boxes and get some weight in the stern!' bellowed Noddy. Brad and Eggo seized the heavy boxes, taking them as far aft as they could. David picked up the big anchor and carried it to the stern, dragging the chain after it. In the wheelhouse Noddy continued to rev the engine but there was no response from the boat, the lightening of her bow not having been enough to release her from the rocks that now gripped her beneath the water.

'You could try swingin' her,' said Noddy. Together the

three of them went first to the starboard side and then to the port, trying to get a good heave on the boat that might just lift her clear of the rocks. It was no use.

'She's hard on,' said Brad.

Noddy switched off the engine. Eggo and David lay on the deck trying to peer into the dark water while Noddy and Brad took a torch and went below to clamber about the bilges looking for signs of damage.

'This is a right bugger of a mess,' Eggo seethed, sitting up and lighting a cigarette. 'What the hell's the old bodach been doin' to get us in a spot like this? He's been working these places for years and he reckons he knows where the rocks are in the sea as well as his wife knows where the pots and pans are in her own kitchen.'

'Maybe he didn't get enough sleep last night,' David said. 'I think he was up playing cribbage for the best part of it.'

'Ach, that bugger doesn't need sleep!' exclaimed Eggo. 'No, he'll be swearin' the boat's done it out of spite for me admirin' that girlie in the magazine, remember?'

The yellow light had left the sky and the horizon was patched with dark wind-ragged clouds that moved too fast. A lighthouse flashed its staccato beams.

Noddy came back. 'She's takin' in water by the stem,' he reported, 'but I can't see any other leaks yet.' There was hope in his voice.

'How fast?' questioned Eggo.

'Fast enough,' admitted Noddy grudgingly.

The lights were put on, making the water look blacker and more sinister in contrast. Brad started the pump.

'How in the hell didn't I know that rock?' Noddy asked brokenly. 'Me, that's been workin' these waters for all the years I've been at sea? I swear I've never come across it in my life before.' He stood on the deck in an agony of bewilderment. 'The bloody bugger of a rock!' he screamed and rushing into the wheelhouse slammed the door after him.

'What's the tide doin'?' asked Eggo practically.

'Dunno,' said Brad. 'Still goin' back, I should think.'

'We'd best get that bugger out of there,' said Eggo. 'We don't want him crackin' up. What's the tide doin'?' he shouted in the direction of the wheelhouse.

Noddy came out, looking at his watch. 'I's got an hour to go yet, I reckon,' he said. Beneath the grey sprouting of beard his face was lined. He seemed to have aged ten years in as many minutes. In the glum silence that ensued they pondered their best course of action. If the *Fair Lassie* was badly holed and if the wind increased with the turning of the tide, as so often happened, the boat would twist and pound, smashing her timbers against the rock. If the tide had more than an hour to go back she was likely to fall right over as the water left her. In that case how did the crew get off?

Selfishly David thought of his own predicament. He reckoned the shore to be a good quarter of a mile away and he had never swum more than fifty yards in his life and that was in the confined water of the town baths. He doubted if he could make fifty yards in this cold water with the amount of sea there was already running. The rest of the crew he knew for certain could not swim a stroke. Not many fishermen could. 'Ach, it takes too long to drown,' they gave as their reason for not learning to swim. David looked around for possible buoyancy aids. There were a couple of lifebuoys hanging beside the wheelhouse but these he had investigated on his first day aboard and found them to be little more than trimly painted canvas bulked out with rotten cork. They were kept there because Noddy thought they improved the appearance of the boat and made no secret of the fact that they would quickly disintegrate once they were in the water. Silently he cursed the stubborn resistance of the fishermen to the carrying of life-saving equipment. 'Ach, it's just a bloody nuisance, and gets in everybody's way,' they objected whenever some authority urged them to take precautions for their own safety. 'There's no room on a working boat for all that stuff,' they would protest and heedlessly take themselves off to do battle with a sea that they knew only too well would be utterly merciless. A recent rumour that the carrying of life-saving equipment was soon to be made compulsory had caused as much indignation as would a rumour that they might be prohibited from carrying a bottle or two of whisky aboard.

David thought fondly of his sister and of how she would receive the news of his death. He thought of his parents and then realising that he was becoming maudlin he briskly nega-tived the thought of drowning by selecting some means of saving his own life and perhaps also the lives of his shipmates.

'Can't we call up one of the other boats on the radio?' asked Eggo. 'They could maybe drag us off.'

'I've been tryin',' Noddy told him. 'But we're screened here by the hills and I don't seem to be able to make any contact.'

David thought he detected the old man wince at the word 'drag' being used in connection with his beloved boat.

'We've got some flares somewhere,' said Brad and jumped down into the hold to reappear a few moments later with a bundle. He lit a flare and its harsh light showed up the wind-whipped silver crests on the steepening ripples.

'She's goin' to start poundin' if it gets much worse than this,' muttered Eggo.

David was almost relieved when the flare died down and shut out the menace of the night.

'I doubt they'll not be seen from here,' mumbled Noddy despairingly. 'Now if I'd gone to the other side of the island like I'd half a mind to at the time. . . .'

'Well, you didn't go, and if you had we wouldn't have been needin' flares very likely,' Eggo cut short Noddy's self-recrimination.

'If she doesn't fall over there's a chance we can float off her at high tide,' said Brad with staunch optimism.

'Oh, aye, no doubt of it at all,' agreed Noddy, though David thought it was with more conviction than he felt.

An empty box slid over from the starboard deck to port. The boat had begun to list, only a little but enough to fill them with increasing dismay. In an effort to help her in her struggle they sat themselves on the starboard gunwale, taking it in turns to go and work the pump.

'Well, we can thank God it's not blowin' up all that fast,' said Noddy. 'She'll be no worse harmed than she is already if it keeps like this.'

'Aye, but is it goin' to keep like this?' Brad asked. No one answered him but the noise of the sea was by no means reassuring.

Crouched against the cold wind they smoked cigarette after cigarette, throwing each glowing stub into the black water. With growing apprehension they adjusted their positions to the increasing list of the boat, and listening to the whimpering of her timbers as the rocks tightened their grip their nerves quivered in sympathy. Repeatedly they asked Noddy the time. Repeatedly they cut short his self-accusation. Eggo lit another flare and by its light they saw that the tide was still ebbing.

Chapter 9

Suddenly David found himself listening intently, thinking he heard the sea-muffled throb of an engine. The others were listening too.

'It's a boat of sorts,' said Eggo eagerly, and simultaneously there appeared the unmistakable glow of a masthead light showing above the peninsula of rocks that marked the north end of the island. The light came out into the open sea. Eggo quickly lit another flare and to their relief the light veered and came towards them. They yelled as the other boat slowed and switched on her floodlight.

Across the stretch of water a voice hailed them:

'Hello! *Spizannah* here! What's the trouble?' It was a deep voice, full of resonance and yet sounding remarkably like a woman's. David was telling himself that their likely rescuer was someone's pleasure yacht when Noddy rejoiced: 'Thank God! It's old *Spizannah*.' He cupped his hand to his mouth.

'Hallo there, *Spizannah*! It's *Fair Lassie* here. We've hit a rock. Fast on. Can you stand by?'

'Aye, How long have you been on?'

'An hour at least.'

'Are you holed?'

'Not badly.'

'I daren't come any closer but the dinghy'll come across.' They heard the splash and rattle of an anchor being

dropped and it was not long before they discerned a dinghy
being paddled towards them. It came alongside. The man in
the dinghy was small and wizened with a dished-in face that
supported a disproportionate amount of nose.

'Aye, aye,' he greeted them calmly.

'Aye, aye,' responded Noddy sounding equally calm.

The man paddled round to their bows and with the aid of a
bright torch made his inspection.

'I don't see much damage and the tide's comin' now. You
should get off by about half-tide,' was his verdict.

'The tide's turned, has it?' Noddy asked.

The man nodded in the direction of his own boat. 'Aye, she
says it just turned and she'll be right about that. The tide
affects her the same as thunder affects some people. She can feel
it in her bones.'

'I daresay we'll lift off then,' said Noddy.

'You'll not need this rope, then?' The little man indicated
a coil of heavy rope that lay in the bottom of the dinghy.

'No, no.' Much of his gloom and fear seemed to have
evaporated now that they had the company of another boat
and his refusal of the rope sounded to David almost abrupt.

'Aye, well,' agreed the man. 'You'll be all right for a while.'
He leaned on his oars. 'She says to come over and have a
drink,' he invited, again nodding in the direction of the other
boat. 'I can only take one at a time in this wee boat, though.'

'I'll not come but you can tell her I thank her just the
same,' said Noddy. 'I'd best stay with the boat.'

Brad spoke up. 'I wouldn't mind comin' over for a dram.'
He looked at Noddy, seeking acquiescence. 'You'll not be
needin' the three of us to stay, will you?'

'No, indeed, but she's best for being lightened of us. Two
had best stay with her though, in case we're needed. You go
and Beardie can go; Eggo and me'll stay with her.'

Brad climbed into the pram and was ferried away. David
turned to Eggo.

'Noddy seems mighty suspicious of the *Spizannah*'s intentions, doesn't he? What's biting him?'

'He'll not let them get a rope aboard, if that's what you mean,' said Eggo. 'Once some of these boats get a rope aboard they can claim part salvage. If they get a man aboard they can claim most of your boat. You have to watch the bastards. Some of 'em are not so much interested in savin' your life as fillin' their own pockets.'

'I hadn't thought of that side of it,' David confessed.

'Well, you need to,' said Noddy, coming up to them. 'If they can get a foot aboard there's one or two of them would not think twice about knockin' you out so as to take over the wheel.'

'What about your chums?' David asked. 'The other fishing boats?'

'Ach, well, now, that's different. They'll help a boat whenever they can. They do it for love of the boats and to help a man out. Mind you, there's one or two of them I wouldn't like to trust further than I could swim.'

'Mind that time we pulled that fellow off the rocks,' Eggo reminded him.

'Aye, I mind fine,' said Noddy. 'That was one of these pleasure boats, not one of ourselves at all. He ran her hard aground on some rocks over the other side. We found her just before the tide left her, listing right over she was and she'd have gone with a mighty thump when she did go. There was a force nine gale forecast at the time and we were in a tear to get the creels lifted before it came but we thought we couldn't leave any boat to suffer a pounding like that. The folks had all got ashore on to some rocks above the tide and they were safe enough, but ach! we felt that sorry for the boat we went in close and got a rope to her somehow. The rope broke twice before we managed to haul her off but we did it at last. Oh, they cheered and shouted and sang when they got aboard her again and found she was all right. Of course we could have claimed a good bit from the insurance for saving her but we were easy and we were in a hurry to get to our creels, so we thought we'd just take what the mannie like to give us himself. He rowed across to us in his dinghy and praised us no end and told us how grateful he was for saving the boat. Then he pulled a pound note out of his wallet. A pound mind you, for saving a couple of thousands pounds worth of boat and a couple of hours hard work for men and boat. "Buy the boys a drink with this, Skipper," he says, "they've done a good job of work today." He thought he was being real generous, too,' finished Noddy with a smile.

'Aye, one bloody quid!' exploded Eggo, obviously still sore at the memory. 'And we could have claimed a few hundred apiece if we'd gone about it the right way.'

'We're not made the right way, thank God,' Noddy told him.

Eggo comforted himself: 'I hope his arsehole festers up and breaks out under his armpits so that he has to take his shirt off every time he wants to have a cac!' he muttered malevolently.

By this time the dinghy had returned for David and as he sat perched on the tiny thwart he remembered where he had seen *Spizannah* before. He climbed on board and his glance fell on a piece of deck cargo that had been stuffed like a large tea-cosy over a stern hatchway. It looked as if it might be a water cylinder in its padded insulation jacket.

The top of the cylinder swivelled round and spoke. David gave a slight start. The voice was the same deep tone that had come pulsating across the water offering aid only a little while before and it came from a prodigiously fat woman with a fat round face and fat round smile, who appeared to be inextricably wedged into the hatchway.

'Welcome aboard, boys,' she called, extending an arm that looked trunk-like beneath the thick fabric of her seaman's jersey across the bosom of which the name 'Spizannah' was spread in white letters made squat by expansion. The grip she had on David's hand would not have shamed an all-in wrestler and it took him so much by surprise that he was almost pulled off his feet as he bent towards her. It was only then he noticed that her long luxuriant hair was loose and cascading over the deck around her. In fact he found he was actually treading on it at one moment and had to step back quickly.

'Let's introduce ourselves, boys, as I don't mind having met you before. This is my boat *Spizannah* as I daresay you've seen for yourselves. I'm her skipper and my name's Spizannah too, but I'm mostly called "Zannah" for short.' It was typical of these sea people that only the boat should be accorded the dignity of her full name. In that élite fraternity mortals must be content with diminutives.

'This here who rowed you over is Mustard, "Mush" for short.'

Brad and David exchanged nods and handshakes with Mush.

'An' do you know why he's called "Mustard"?' Zannah demanded with a great gurgle of laughter. 'My late husband christened him that because he said he was no use unless he was fresh every morning. Isn't that right, Mush?' She rolled her remarkably large eyes at Mush so that the whites glistened in the lamplight. Mush grinned at her devotedly. 'Ten hours' sleep Mush must have out of every twenty-four or he's as stale as horse-piss and useless for work. See he gets his proper sleep and Mush's as good after it as Popeye after spinach. Tackle anything, he will. That's true, isn't it, Mush? I'm tellin' no lie, am I, Mush?' There was even more devotion in Mush's vigorously nodded affirmation.

Brad, who had been waiting on deck all this time, started to blow on his cupped hands and to rub them together. David was feeling the cold more in his feet and began stumping them on the deck, wondering gloomily if their hostess was jammed so tightly in the hatchway that they would have to take their promised drams up there in the open. The light coming up through the glass decklight was enticing and the smoke from the 'Charlie Noble' chimney was making warm prophecies. They were delighted therefore when after a final scrutiny of the *Fair Lassie*'s position Zannah said at last, 'Well, come on below, boys. No use standing about up here getting your death.' She gave her body an experimental heave, belched a couple of times, which seemed to reduce her bulk sufficiently for her to begin extricating herself, and then wriggling and manoeuvring her vast bust with both hands she lowered herself through the hatchway, pulling her hair in after her. Gratefully Brad and David followed. Mush came down last and shut the hatch after him.

It was good to be in the cosy safeness of a fo'c'sle once more, and *Spizannah*'s fo'c'sle was such a revelation in the way of colour and comfort that David and Brad snatched off their caps as if they were entering a drawing room. The portholes were outlined with gaily striped curtains; the floor was carpeted; every visible piece of metal or woodwork shone with polish and the forward door had a sparkling glass handle. David and Brad sat down on a resilient bunk that was covered in a deep blue fabric. Opposite them there was a similar bunk above which a recessed shelf held a sedate row of books. Fastened to one bulkhead there was a gilt-framed mirror, flanked by a couple of arrestingly vivid oil paintings, though these frivolities were opposed on the other bulkhead by a solidly efficient barometer and a sternly vigilant ship's clock. David was enchanted and tried hard to memorise every detail of it for the time when he should aspire to his own boat.

Zannah opened a small cupboard on her right and took out a bottle of whisky and five glasses.

'You going to have a drink with us, Mush?' she asked. Mush gestured a refusal. 'I'll get to my kip,' he muttered and immediately disappeared through a door leading aft.

'He'll have a couple of hours now and then he'll get up again to see you safely off,' Zannah explained as she captured her flowing hair, twisted it into a hawser-thick rope and flung it negligently behind her. 'An' I'll tell you this for true, boys,' she went on. 'If you was to get up and follow him out now, this minute, you wouldn't get a word of sense out of Mush, you wouldn't, for once he's made up his mind to kip he's deep asleep before ever he climbs into his bunk.' She laughed, a deeply reverberant laugh that pulled at the muscles of her stomach so that it jigged up and down like a toy on a length of elastic. In the midst of her quaking she returned the fifth glass to the cupboard. David was wondering why she should still leave four when she raised her voice.

'Spice!' she called. 'Spice! Come and help me entertain. Don't you know we've got company?'

David and Brad turned to each other with half-delighted, half-abashed grins as a feminine voice answered from beyond the glass-handled door. Brad jumped up, smoothed his sideboards in front of the mirror and scrubbed a despairing hand over a chin that looked as spiky as dead gorse.

'This is my niece,' said Zannah. 'She's called "Spizannah" as well as myself and the boat, so we have to call her "Spice" for short. Come on, Spice. Come and be introduced.'

The girl who came through the door stood leaning against it, assessing them briefly before coming forward to accept their proffered hands. David heard Brad draw in an appreciative breath and she flicked him an amused look that dropped him back into his seat open-mouthed with astonishment. She turned her attention to David.

'I've seen you before,' she told him. 'Where?'

'Where?' David was confused.

'I was swabbing the deck and you threw a dead crab at me,' she said.

'It wasn't me,' David denied. 'It was one of the kids.'

'Oh yes,' she said disbelievingly.

'Honest,' said David. 'They took you for a boy, though. I did myself at first.'

'Well, you don't think so now, do you?' said Zannah.

The amused smile was still in Spice's eyes as she looked up at David.

He could have sworn that at that moment the boat gave a sudden lurch and that the hand he put out to grasp hers was put out involuntarily to steady himself. But neither Spice nor the other two seemed to have noticed any unusual movement and he saw that the whisky in the glasses had stayed level and still. He found himself staring down into eyes that were blue-grey with gold flecks in them, like a tranquil sea splashed with sunset. They had the witchery of the sea in them too; witchery and beguilement and smiles.

'Haven't you another name besides "Beardie"?' she was asking.

'Well, yes.' David swallowed. 'David. Dave for short.' Already his real name had begun to sound strange and unused.

'Hello, Dave,' Spice said. 'Nice to meet you.'

They all drank a glass of whisky and it steadied David enough for him to take in that Spice had mahogany-red hair that fell to her shoulders; that her eyes were made emphatic by the sleek black brows that were poised as if to take flight at any moment; that she was below average height and that she was a little on the plump side. The sort of figure, he thought, that emaciated women would describe as 'stocky'.

'Now, Spice, these boys will be hungry. Go and get a bite of something for them to eat,' Zannah instructed.

'I have it ready,' said Spice and went out into the galley. She returned with two dishes, one piled high with cheese sandwiches, the other covered by a sugared pastry crust. The sight of the food reminded them of their hunger and David stretched out an eager hand. As he did so Spice looked down, smiling directly at him. He forgot the food, he forgot the presence of Brad and Zannah, as their eyes held each other's for one glorious spinning moment.

Oh God! he thought, with a mixture of sadness and elation. This is it. This is my enchanted evening.

Chapter 10

Fair Lassie came off with comparative ease two hours after low tide. *Spizannah* stood by as Noddy started the engine and steered cautiously into the shelter of the cove. The crew were elated to feel the boat responding once again to the lift of the water after the hours of imprisonment on the rock.

'We'll put her ashore in the river here as soon as it's light enough,' said Noddy, appraising the thinning darkness. 'We'll see what's the damage then, and maybe get her off in time for haulin' if she's fit enough.'

Eggo brought up some sturdy pit props from the hold and they lashed them below the rubbing-band so that when the boat was put ashore they would act as stays to prevent her falling over. *Spizannah* waited offshore until *Fair Lassie* was safely in the river and the tide had gone down enough for any damage to become visible. They paddled around in the river inspecting her hull.

'It's the keel that's taken most of it,' Noddy declared, 'and the iron's saved that, but there's a fair rub on a couple of her planks here on the port side.' They stood looking at the patch of rough, splintered wood left by the rocks. 'We can soon put a tingle over that,' Noddy added.

'If that's all that's wrong, where's the water gettin' in?'

demanded Brad, evidently suspicious that Noddy was glossing over the damage so as to continue fishing. 'All that water in the boat hasn't been comin' in through a rub.'

'Ach, she's lost a good bit of caulkin', that's what that trouble is,' Noddy allowed. 'We can hammer a bit of caulkin' into the seams and she'll be tight enough yet.'

'Where are we goin' to get caulkin'?' Brad enquired cynically. 'There's none on the boat so far as I know.'

'There is so.' Noddy was confident.

Eggo pulled a knife from his pocket. 'What the hell are we worryin' about caulkin' for when there's a black hairy bugger like old Beardie here aboard the boat? Come here, you great slob!' He rushed towards David, brandishing the knife as if he were about to cut off his beard. David dodged, yelled and ran splashing through the river to the other side of the boat to escape him, and they indulged in some minutes of horseplay until Eggo lost his foothold on the slippery stones and together they landed, one on top of the other, in the river. Seeing them spluttering and struggling Brad and Noddy burst out laughing and suddenly they were all bent double with laughter, their spirits light again after the tension of the night.

Confidently they gave *Spizannah* the 'thumbs-up' sign which she acknowledged with a raucous bellow of her klaxon. They watched the sweeping curve of her wake as she started out of the bay. Zannah herself, her hair piled inside a large plastic bag, lifted an arm in salute and they heard a snatch of song wafted to them across the water. Amidships Spice was waving concentratedly. They pulled off their 'toories' and waved with an exuberance that made David, for some obscure reason, feel slightly treacherous. *Spizannah* went out of sight around the headland and only a curl of water and a couple of dispassionate gulls marked her wake.

'You've fairly made a hit there,' said Brad enviously.

David grinned happily. 'I believe I have.'

'He'll do well enough for himself if he gets that one,' said Noddy. 'Zannah's one that'll not want for anythin' so long as she lives and I daresay the lassie'll get the lot of it.'

'She's a bloody good-looker,' said Brad.

'She's a bloody fine woman, is Zannah,' went on Noddy, misinterpreting Brad's allusion. 'She doesn't need to go runnin' a cargo boat to make her livin'. She could have retired when her husband died for the matter of that, but ach, Zannah's one that seems she canna abide the smell of the land.'

'Beardie's not interested in Zannah, you dirty old man,' Brad told him. 'It's Spice he's makin' a line for.'

'I don't see the use in her,' Eggo put in. 'You want to get somebody a bit handier. When do you think you're going to have your fun with her?'

'You didn't see her properly,' David told him. 'Wait till I take her to the dance on Saturday night. *Spizannah*'s making for the harbour now and Spice has promised to come with me. It's all fixed up.'

'You lucky bastard!' said Brad. He swung himself aboard to get hammer and nails and a tingle while the others teased out the caulking Noddy had produced and hammered it into the seams. When at last the tingle was on and they had daubed it liberally with tar they went aboard to wait for the tide to come up far enough to test the success of their repairs and eventually to refloat the boat. With the floorboards up they crouched in the bilges watching intently for the first trickles or gouts of water that would betray a leak. There were none, and Noddy, after a spell of cogitation, decided that she was making no more water than was customary.

'Are we all fit, then?' he asked lightheartedly.

'All fit', the crew assured him of their preparedness.

It was raining now—heavy, squally rain that swept up the cove like a wide, wind-whipped skirt. The noise of it hitting the sea came first as a sizzling sound which grew to a roar as it overwhelmed them, spattering the deck with globules the size of egg-yolks which in turn were picked up by the wind and harried over the gunwale and through the scuppers.

'It's lookin' pretty coarse out there,' Noddy warned. 'I'm thinkin' we'll need the mizzen for haulin'. Best get it up now, don't you think, boys?'

Brad muttered. Eggo swore. The mizzen was the heaviest of storm canvas. They unlashed it from the mizzen-boom and hoisted it on the halyard. 'Sweat it up tight,' Noddy adjured them.

'Okay!' they shouted when they had done.

'Okay, we'll press on, then.' He went into the wheelhouse and with the waxing confidence of a convalescent after illness *Fair Lassie* took joyously to the water again.

It was by now the afternoon of Friday and first thing Saturday morning they had to be back in port with the catch of lobsters boxed and ready for the buyers. They knew they were in for a long and difficult haul, for the storm lanterns Noddy had seen in the sky the previous night had been true harbingers. As soon as they got out from the lee of the island the seas came in rolling white-capped masses that broke constantly over the bows, crashed against the wheelhouse and streamed along the deck. Noddy, determined to get as many of the creels lifted as he could in the daylight that was left eased off the engine only for the biggest seas. Eggo and Brad were squeezed into the wheelhouse along with him and David, finding there was no room for him, went down to the fo'c'sle and put on a kettle, holding it steady on the stove as it boiled. As soon as the tea was brewed he signalled the others who took it in turns to come down and drink mugs of it along with hurried mouthfuls of bread and jam before rushing back to keep watch in the wheelhouse. Their last meal had been breakfast on Thursday morning yet there were no complaints of hunger. They were intent on finding the creel floats hidden among the rioting seas, and hunger and weariness had been forgotten.

By the time darkness came they had found and lifted most of the creels and taken them to quiet water to lie for the weekend. The weather was worsening; the boat covering herself with spray.

'How many more fleets yet?' David asked, shielding his face from the hailstones which were hitting him with such persistent accuracy he felt like a number on a dartboard.

'Two yet,' Brad gasped. He and David crowded into the wheelhouse with Noddy while Eggo cowered behind it. In the light from the decklamps the sea lunged and foamed around the boat, shutting out the sound of the wind with its own turbulence. The heavy mizzen banged from side to side, shuddering the whole boat.

Eggo opened the door. 'Enough's enough,' he complained. 'We'll never be able to see the buoys tonight anyway.'

'We put a danbuoy on this next lot.' Noddy was unrelenting. 'Surely we'll get a chance to see it if we put out the lights.'

The lights went out and David and Brad joined Eggo on the deck to peer into the darkness in the hope of discerning the pennanted spike of the danbuoy over the trough of a wave. The boat heaved and wallowed as Noddy brought her round. They were all aware of the risk of getting the rope caught in the propeller. A fouled propeller in this sea would imperil boat and crew.

Suddenly Brad shouted and pointed. His night-trained eyes had spotted the buoy well inside where Noddy had judged it would be found. The boat rolled towards it as Eggo and Brad grabbed a boathook each, the one ready in case the other should miss hooking it. Eggo got it and Brad ran back to the winch. Drenched with spray and with water sluicing round their feet they worked along the line of creels. The boat was listing to the pull of the fleet and at the same time bucking and tossing.

'Take the next one!' Eggo commanded David and jumped into the hold to shift the dripping creels around.

'Never mind that! Throw the buggers in anyhow but just keep haulin'. Keep haulin', you bastards!' Noddy's bellow brought Eggo leaping back to his place.

The physical effort of fighting the boat as she tried to fling them one way or another was immense. David could think of nothing but keeping his foothold as he hauled, and extracted and stowed the lobsters.

The wheelhouse window opened. 'Hang on, boys!' roared Noddy peremptorily and immediately they all flung their arms round the staunch strength of the lowered mast as a big sea swept over the boat. Noddy in the protection of the wheelhouse was the only one who could give any attention to the sea.

'Watch it!' Again his yell sent them clinging to the mast as the boat took another lump of solid water. Eggo lost his hold for a moment and was flung against the winch.

The buoy at the end of the fleet came up and if David had had any breath he might have cheered. He had forgotten that there was still another fleet to haul before they finished. With lights off again the boat pounded into the sea as they tried to locate the buoy.

'It must be somewhere here,' said Noddy after he had turned for the tenth time and still they had not found it.

'It must have sunk,' suggested Brad.

'Ach no.' Noddy was obdurate. He turned the boat round yet again.

Eggo lost patience. 'Ach, come on you old bodach. Let's leave it where it is. That's Saturday mornin' comin' over the hills back there and we'll miss the market with the lobsters we have got if you spend any more time lookin' for this lot.'

David glanced back over his shoulder to where a paling of the sky showed a hesitant dawn.

'We'll just have one more run,' insisted Noddy. 'And if we don't get it this time we'll leave it.'

Again David forced his eyes to peer through the dark, reflecting cynically on the comparative indolence of lobster fishing in the *Silver Spray* and recalling the odds and ends of old cork which Donald deemed sufficient to buoy his creels; the few dozen lobsters which they had extolled as a worth-while week's work; the unashamed run for home when the sea looked too threatening. Already in the short time he had been aboard the *Fair Lassie* he felt he had become a more competent mariner than Donald himself.

In spite of the concentrated staring of four pairs of eyes the buoy of the last fleet eluded them. The decklights flashed on again as Noddy turned homeward and opened the throttle. Brad, Eggo and David muttered together with relief. By this time they were all at the teeth-chattering stage of cold and dazed with an exhaustion that was as much due to keeping their balance as to the exertion of hauling. Noddy, relatively snug in his wheelhouse, was the only one who showed signs of resentment at having to abandon the search for the buoy.

Brad and Eggo set about the task of 'stabbing' the sinews of the lobsters' claws before packing them into boxes. David went below and made more tea, buttered more chunks of bread and spread them with jam before he called them down. They ate abstractedly, as men do when they are as eager to satisfy their need for warmth as to satisfy their hunger.

Eggo said: 'I got a bashin' when I hit that winch. My back's fairly sore after it.'

'Is that what's bitin' you?' asked Brad. 'I thought there must be somethin'. What d'you reckon you've done, slipped a disc?'

'Maybe,' admitted Eggo.

'Well, in that case you'd best not go to the doctor with it,' Brad warned him. 'He'll only send you to the hospital like they sent Harry. They played about with him for months without puttin' him right.'

'He seems all right now,' Eggo pointed out. 'He's back at the fishin', isn't he?'

'Aye, he's fine now but it wasn't the hospital that put him right. It was a fellow in Glasgow that did it. And in five minutes, so Harry says.'

'Five minutes?' repeated Eggo sceptically and groaned as he tried to straighten himself.

'Aye, it's true! Harry said he just sat him down on a chair and twisted his head round and round till it hurt like hell. Then he says to Harry, "Now, what I'm goin' to do to you now will hurt you a little bit," and before Harry had time to make up his mind to let himself be hurt the fellow grabbed hold of his head and gave it such a twist Harry swears his face went right round to the back of his neck. He says the pain was like a flash of fire. He thought he'd exploded and was dead, but the next minute the man said, "You can get up now", and Harry felt fine. He's never had a twinge from his slipped disc since. You can see that for yourself.'

Eggo swallowed hard. 'And you say I should go and have my head twisted round to the back of my neck to cure me?' he expostulated. 'Ach, to hell with that. I don't want to waste my time strugglin' to reach down the back of my trousers every time I want to piss.'

Noddy refused to leave the wheelhouse to come for tea and David, half blinded by spray, staggered along the deck to take him tea in a can and bread and butter wrapped in a sugar bag. Noddy snatched careful mouthfuls of tea between pulling at the helm.

Once in the wheelhouse David stayed listening to the chat coming over the radio. Dawn had come grudgingly, revealing the sea as a chaos of grey and white with monster fanged waves curling at *Fair Lassie*'s stern before smashing down into the troughs she had just vacated.

'The *Ocean Princess* has been up round Cape Wrath for a couple of weeks and is comin' in with twenty-six boxes,' Noddy told him. 'Now that's good fishin' for you. I'm thinkin' though they'll have taken a bad tearin' comin' all that way through this weather,' he comforted himself.

They listened for more reports. 'That's not so good,' commented Noddy of one. 'That'll no more than pay for his fuel.'

Though they knew from the radio they were only one of a company of boats all making for port they saw no sign of any of them, the towering waves and the white mist of spray enclosing them in a world of their own.

'Another half hour and we'll be in the calmer water,' Noddy promised confidently.

'I didn't feel sick through it all,' David pointed out, in case Noddy had missed the phenomenon.

'Aye, I'm surprised at that. There's plenty would have been spewing their insides up in weather like this and them folks as is more used to the sea than you are.'

David himself was astonished that he had felt no twinge of queasiness even when preparing food down in the stuffiness of the fo'c'sle. It put the accolade on his decision to become a fisherman.

'Not that seasickness will harm anybody,' continued Noddy 'Take Brad, now, he's sick as a dog every time we get a bit of a blow. I mind a fellow who lives in the port there who's only a summer sailor. Every back end he puts his boat ashore and doesn't take her out till well on in the spring. The first week he's out he's sick until he gets used to her again. But he just says it does him good to be sick. He swears he feels better all the summer for it. I can well believe him, too. A good dose of seasickness is better than any medicine.'

'Hallo, hallo, hallo, there, Cassie my girl. Jim speaking. Come on now. Get that bloke out of your bed, I'll be back in the house in an hour.' The deep baritone of a skipper crackled over the radio, filling the wheelhouse with the sound.

David looked enquiringly at Noddy. 'All the wives have trawler-band radios and listen in for when their men are comin' home,' he explained. The voice went on to retail the news of the week's fishing.

'Get off now, Jim, while I talk to my Jessie,' another voice pleaded, and so it went on as the men warned their wives of their homecoming.

By the time David left the wheelhouse to go back to the fo'c'sle the sea was much chastened and they were able to glimpse the dark mass of the mainland between successive shrouds of rain. He found Eggo irritably clearing up. In a bucket had been dumped the perishable food remaining from the week's supplies. Sausages and meat—smelling a little by this time; a couple of wrapped loaves; a squashed paper of butter; a sadly damp packet of cigarettes. Eggo picked up the two tea-towels they had used and bundling them together threw them on top of the bucket.

'Ditch that lot,' he instructed David.

'What? The tea-towels too?'

'Aye.'

'Can't you wash them out or get the laundry to do it?'

'No need. We have a regular order for two new ones every week.'

'What a waste,' David commented. 'It wouldn't cost much to get them washed and they'd last for weeks then.'

'Ditch them, I said,' Eggo repeated. 'Talk about mean English slobs.'

'Welsh,' corrected David.

'Same thing,' said Eggo.

David did as he was told and watched a gull pitting itself against the wind as it tried to land on the water.

'What's the objection to sending tea-towels to the laundry?' he pursued when he returned.

'You wouldn't get me eatin' and drinkin' from dishes that had been wiped with a laundry-washed cloth,' answered Eggo. 'We might be only common fishermen but we like a bit of hygiene just the same.'

'Like spitting in the chip fat,' David reminded him mischievously.

Eggo ignored him and glared at the clock above the bunks. 'Look at that,' he grumbled. 'We wouldn't have wasted time lookin' for that last bloody buoy if I'd had my way. I knew we'd never see it.'

'What's all the hurry?' David asked. 'We're making good enough time now, aren't we?'

'Good enough for you lot but I've got to get back to the house, take my dinner and get all toffeed up in time to catch the train at half past eleven.'

'Meeting someone?' David let the table flaps down.

'No bloody fear,' said Eggo 'I'm away to collect my new suit. They promised they'd have it ready for me today.' He bundled up some old papers and threw them out of the hatch. 'I'm thinkin' of wearin' it for the dance tonight so you can keep your eye open and tell me how I look in it.' He popped his head out of the hatch to make sure the papers had cleared the deck. 'I thought as much.' His voice was disgruntled. 'We're just about the last lobster boat in.'

The harbour, half enclosed by the hills, was sheltered from the worst of the wind and they entered it to an explosive charivari of gulls. Noddy sent Brad to peal the harbour bell to attract the attention of buyers while David and Eggo unloaded the week's catch. Immediately they had finished a swarm of children descended on the boat, intent on salvaging any empty bottles on which they could collect a few pence.

'How're we doin'?' Eggo asked when Noddy and Brad returned.

'No' bad, no' bad,' replied Noddy, looking pleased.

Eggo muttered a perfunctory farewell and rushed off homewards. Brad, with a 'See you Monday, then,' and a flick of his smile strolled away along the pier, his progress punctuated by brief discussions with other crews. Noddy called David into the fo'c'sle.

'You'll be coming out with us next week?' The note of enquiry was only a politeness.

'That'll suit me fine,' David told him gratefully.

'Aye well. Might just as well see the season out with us if you've nothin' better to do,' Noddy said. He pulled out a bundle of notes. 'Here's a pound for yourself, then, boy.'

David gaped at the number of notes Noddy was pushing into his hand, but when he was about to protest Noddy insisted, 'No, no. It's your share, we're all agreed. You've earned it.'

David was embarrassed. He had enjoyed a week's good fishing and a lavish dose of excitement. He hadn't expected to be paid as well.

'Look, Noddy,' he said seriously, 'I'm not as short as all that. I've still a few pounds in the Post Office and I was intending to get some out today.'

Noddy picked up his pipe and tobacco and stuffed them into his pocket. 'Aye well, throw it over the side if you've no use for it,' he said indifferently. 'But next week, if it's a poor week, there may be nothin' at all for you, so you'd best hang on to it.' He climbed out of the fo'c'sle, leaving David smiling affectionately at his handful of notes—his first earnings from the sea. He stuffed them into his shirt pocket and felt as if he was wearing a medal.

He followed Noddy up on to the pier, and wandered about watching the catches of other boats being loaded on to lorries that then went grinding heavily up the hill with their slimy dripping loads.

A cheerful figure carrying a brand-new coil of rope over his arm accosted him. 'How're you gettin' on with the fishin'?'

'Fine,' responded David. 'Suits me down to the ground.'

The man raised an amused eyebrow. 'Well, down to sea-level if you prefer it that way,' David corrected.

'Aye, aye. Fishin's a good life, no doubt of that,' he agreed. 'Maybe we don't make much money but we do have fun.' He plodded away.

Just in front of the railway station Eggo appeared. Shaved and 'toffeed up' in sports jacket, flannels and with his shoes brightly polished he could have passed for the complete landsman. Only the folded raincoat which, though it was raining quite heavily, he carried neatly folded over one arm betrayed the fact that he was accustomed to being encased in more adequate clothing.

'You've been quick,' David called to him. 'You must have swallowed your dinner like a boa constrictor.'

Eggo paused briefly. 'Dinner!' came the bitter retort. 'I didn't have time to take my dinner. All I did was to take a run round the table and a kick at the cat.' His short legs broke into a run as a long shrill whistle came from inside the station.

David bought himself some steak to eat over the weekend and then was tempted into buying half a dozen cakes. He bought fruit too to counteract the stodginess of the week's diet. The girl in the fruit shop was dark eyed and full-busted with the perfect complexion which appears to be a birthright of all Highland women. Her mouth fascinated him by its minuteness and by the perfection of its shape; it was, he thought, the nearest thing to the poetic rosebud that he had ever seen. Simply to satisfy his male egotism he indulged in a mild flirtation with her and was gratified to see that she reacted with flushing cheeks and fluttering eyelids. But, he noticed with amusement, the rosebud mouth did not once burgeon into bloom.

At the ship chandler's he invested in an oilskin and sou'-wester and a pair of thigh boots, for he was still wearing the clothes from the boat's store. He also bought a pair of jeans and on the crew's recommendation a pair of 'long-johns'. The idea of swaddling his lower limbs in such a garment would, a week ago, have struck him as ludicrous but the experience of the last two nights had shown him how cold deck work could be. With winter only at the stage of licking its chops he deemed it wiser to bow to the voice of experience.

With almost no money left but satisfied that now he would be adequately clad for the life at sea he returned to the *Fair Lassie*. He had contemplated paying a call on the *Spizannah* which he had located up at the top of the harbour but she was still amid the hullaballoo of unloading and he guessed his presence might be unwelcome. He had watched covertly from behind one of the curing sheds but as neither Zannah nor Spice had appeared on deck he gathered they would be fully occupied down below or else they were ashore somewhere.

On board he boiled a kettle and washed out his dirty underwear while the steak cooked. After dinner he washed himself thoroughly—his first wash for over a week—before he set the alarm clock for six o'clock and getting into his bunk gave himself up to the prospect of a few hours sleep before it would be time to spruce himself up in readiness to take Spice to the dance. He had forgotten, however, that the children would be coming to deliver the supplies and was jerked into consciousness after only about half an hour by the banging open of the hatch. After their first querulous surprise at finding him there they accepted his sleepy mumblings as an exhortation to go away. They dumped the boxes and David heard the hatch bang down as they left. He was almost asleep again when he heard a young voice shrill out to its companions: 'That bearded chappie is still asleep down there. You'd think he had no home to go to.'

Chapter 11

Spizannah, portholes aglow, lay alongside the pier, her mast swinging gently to the motion of the swell. The busy smoke from the galley chimney was tinged with the smell of baking. David opened the hatch and called and immediately Zannah's voice responded, bidding him to come down. Zannah, wearing a large floral overall and with her hair confined in a Gurkha-like turban, was seated at the table patting a round of oatcakes into shape. There were more oatcakes already crisp and cooling on a tray. David had just eaten several rounds of bread and cheese and three of the half dozen cakes he had bought but when Zannah put out a butter dish and, indicating the oatcakes, invited him to help himself he could not resist. His mouth was full and there were crumbs and melted butter on his beard when Spice appeared.

'Hallo!' she said, and gave him a warm, amused smile.

Self-consciously David wiped the crumbs from his beard. He had been worried while he was dressing that all he had to wear for the dance was his jeans and thick sweater so that he was relieved to see that Spice was wearing a plain skirt topped by a blouse and woollen cardigan.

'Are you fit?' he asked her, getting up.

'I'm fit,' she replied, pulling on a coat.

He followed her up the steps and on to the pier, taking a proprietory grasp of her arm as they left the few yards of

metalled road to cross a wooden bridge over a burn and subsequently to pick their way along a muddy path. The corrugated iron shed where the dance was being held loomed
before them like an abandoned warehouse. There was no
sound distinguishable above the noise of the wind and rain
and the only light visible was a glimmer above the doorway
which did its sad best to illumine the two rough steps that
marked the entrance.

'I wonder if they've started yet?' Spice's voice sounded
dubious.

'Oh, surely,' David told her, although his own doubt
matched hers. 'It was supposed to have started more than an
hour ago.'

'That means nothing in these parts,' she murmured.

Two youths engaged in exclamatory conversation thudded
out of the darkness from the opposite direction and bounded
up the steps to the hall. David and Spice followed them into
a musty smelling porch, blinking the rain from their eyelashes
in the glare of an unshaded bulb. The doorkeeper hailed them
companionably, took their money and counted change while
thrusting acrid taunts into the conversation the two youths
were still pursuing. Spice went to dispose of her coat and
David was directed to go through a pair of swing doors into
the dance hall. Here more unshaded bulbs hung from the low
trusses above which was the apex of the iron roof. He saw
through a haze of cigarette smoke that the floor was of plain
wood, dusty and splintery, and that the walls were also wood
but that they had been varnished to a sticky looking kipper
goldness. The men were bunched along the length of one
wall: a proportion of them had shaved, wore their best suits or
else flannels and sweaters and light, shiny shoes. The rest wore
jeans and sweaters and scabby shoes that looked as if they
might have been fished out of the harbour for the occasion.
Not having bothered to change they had not bothered to
shave off their week's growth of beard, 'shaving' being for the

fishermen synonymous with changing. All of the men looked ill at ease and were paying exaggerated attention to the lighting of their cigarettes or else were pretending to be involved in serious discussion, anything in fact rather than appear to be paying attention to the girls who were ranged along the opposite wall. Across from where David stood awaiting Spice's reappearance there was a raised platform on which a three piece band sat poised as if ready to strike up the music. There appeared to be some sort of hitch, however, for though everyone waited with obvious expectancy the signal to start dancing did not come.

A hand clapped David's shoulder. 'Come on and have a wee dram to start you off,' entreated Brad's voice. His breath was already whisky-flavoured.

'Not yet,' David declined. 'I'm waiting for someone.' He winked at Brad. 'Don't you remember?'

'Ach, come on,' Brad exhorted. 'You canna dance on an empty stomach, man. Anyway, it'll be a while before the next dance starts.'

'Why?' asked David, yielding and following Brad into the men's lavatory where it transpired all the serious drinking of the evening was to take place. 'What's causing all the delay?'

'They've just taken the M.C. out at the back to try will they sober him up so that he can start announcing again,' Brad explained. 'They say they'll have to throw a bucket of water over him this time.'

It was some minutes later that, enlivened by a couple of drams, David returned to the dance floor to be greeted by a faintly disapproving Spice. The eyes of the dancers were by then turned towards the platform on to which a white-faced young man, buttressed on either side by the sturdy shoulder of an accomplice, was making an unsteady ascent. His hair hung damply over his forehead and the knees of his trousers were mudstained, betraying the fact that his friends had contrived to bring him to this degree of sobriety only by forcing him to kneel down beside the burn and then ducking his head into it. In a strident voice he bade his audience take their partners for a 'Gay Gordons' and, being instantly deserted by his two accomplices who were rivals for the same dancing partner, he teetered forward and pitched over the front of the platform. Amid shouts of laughter the band struck up and, ignoring the still prostrate M.C., the more ebullient males rushed at the ranks of girls. The rest of the men evinced little interest in the proceedings with the result that though the girls were outnumbered by two to one many of them were left partnerless. With placid independence they got up and danced together. When the 'Gay Gordons' had come to an end it was judged that the M.C. was incapable of further duties and so the doorkeeper between visits to the men's lavatory announced the dances. Eventually, however, he too succumbed and thereafter it was left to the dancers to deduce from the music which dance they should embark on.

It was past midnight before a splendidly attired Eggo made his self-conscious appearance, but the acquisition of a new suit plus the consumption of several drams seemed to have given him enough confidence to venture on to the dance floor. Contrary to his assertion to David that he could not dance he was soon indulging in a spirited 'Dashing White Sergeant' and hauling his two partners around the floor with as much puffing and breathing as affected him when he was hauling a fleet of creels out of a rough sea.

'Have you seen our Eggo tonight?' Brad's voice hailed David from the midst of a bevy of girls who had festooned themselves round his chair in a way that reminded David of pictures he had seen of Edwardian chorus girls clustering around a magnanimous backer. 'He's fairly enjoyin' himself tonight.'

Spice set herself the task of teaching David some of the Highland dances and together they romped around the floor until suddenly realising that it was past two o'clock she said:

'Aunt Zannah sleeps in the fo'c'sle and won't be able to go to bed until you've gone, so if you want a bite of supper with us we'd best go now.'

The rain was still pelting down as they ran hand in hand down to the pier and climbed aboard *Spizannah*. There on deck, swaying to the motion of the boat, they clung together for a few precious seconds. At last Spice pushed him away.

'Your beard's all wet,' she complained and put her hands over her face. He pulled them away and held on. 'Come on, let's go below,' she urged. 'The rain's running down the neck of my blouse.'

'Lucky rain,' David murmured, his mouth pulling at a wet tendril of hair that was not confined by her head scarf.

'Oh, do come on,' she insisted. 'Your trousers will be so wet you won't be allowed to sit on the bunk.'

He let go her hands. 'I wouldn't object to taking them off,' he whispered, kissing the rain from her face.

Spice chuckled. 'Aunt Zannah would have something to say about that, and maybe I'd object too.' Playfully she grasped a handful of his beard and pulled. He gripped both her wrists strengthening his grip until she had released her hold and was begging for mercy.

'Monster!' she taunted.

'Virago!' he gave back.

Laughingly she evaded his arms and opened the hatch. He followed, close enough to have to step carefully for fear of treading on her hands as she let herself down. They were still laughing when they reached the fo'c'sle where Zannah was sitting with her elbows on the table and her hair, grey-streaked in the lamplight, cascading on to the bunk. She was chewing at a pencil but she took it from her mouth to make room for the smile that lit up her face in response to the gaiety Spice and David had brought with them. As he wiped the rain from his hair and beard with a towel Spice had handed him David studied Zannah furtively. Was there ever such a woman, he wondered, with her strong good looks, her bulk and her air of buoyant serenity that made one think of her as being permanently cushioned on a cloud of goodwill towards her fellow men. Some day, David promised himself, he would ask Spice about her. Noddy had been able to tell him little except that when she was in her 'teens Zannah was supposed to have run away with the rollicking, rumbustious Irishman she had later married, and that the couple had started off with a small fishing boat carrying cargo to ports not served by the regular steamers and had prospered well enough to buy *Spizannah* and have her converted to their own requirements. The husband had been drowned some ten years ago. It was said that he had fallen into the harbour after a heavy Saturday night ashore with friends. Since then Zannah had carried on the cargo running alone except for the aid of 'Mush', who she and her husband were supposed to have rescued from an attempt at suicide after his wife had left him.

Zannah was looking at David. 'That's a mighty good beard you have there,' she remarked with admiration. 'Did it take you long to grow it?'

David, trying to recollect just how long, said, 'No, not very long.'

She beckoned him to lean closer so that she could see it, and taking it in the palm of her hand she inspected it, David thought like a health visitor might inspect a child's head for nits. 'Aye,' she murmured approvingly. 'It's a good quality, too.' She released her hold. 'Now my husband had a beard—a real rusty red one it was, but coarse! It was that coarse you could have scraped the barnacles off the boat with it. And when he got older it didn't get a grey hair in it. No, never a one, but it got a bit straggly. He got to look as if he was goin' about chewin' at a mouthful of dead bracken all the time.'

'If it was as coarse as all that, it must have been a b it un
comfortable,' suggested David.

'Uncomfortable. It was purgatory for me sometimes. He
was the hairiest man you'd ever see. All over his chest and his
back it was too. And that strong when he lay on you it was
like cuddlin' a gorse bush. I'm tellin' you, he never could
wear a shirt more than three days without the back being
rubbed out of it.' Her eyes softened at some memory, and
then she said suddenly: 'It was bloody expensive.'

Spice took a tablecloth from one of the lockers and spread
it on the table. With a sigh Zannah gathered up a galaxy of
coloured pamphlets from which she had been copying information into a hard-backed notebook. David was astonished
to see that they were rose catalogues and gardening magazines.

'Gardening?' he asked facetiously.

'Aye, that's about the way of it,' Zannah replied without a
trace of embarrassment.

David looked enquiringly at Spice.

'Aunt Zannah always gets out her rose catalogues when
she's stuck in port,' Spice explained. 'She's a real expert on
roses, aren't you, Aunt Zannah?'

Zannah shut the catalogues into a locker. 'I reckon I know
a fair bit about them, anyway,' she admitted.

'Did you have a garden at some time?' David probed.

'No, I never have, boy. I'll tell you the truth, the nearest
I've ever got to gardenin' was havin' a bumble bee fly down
the front of my dress.' Her chuckle burst out from the back
of her throat and her belly and bust started their private war
of laughter. She controlled herself long enough to add, 'Right
down, it went.' She pulled at the throat of her dress and
chuckled again. Spice poured out a cup of tea and put it in
front of her aunt. Zannah took a sip and then after a clearing
burst of laughter went on.

'You see, when the bee got me I was sittin' in the hatch

eatin' a plate of jam puddin'. Well, I'm a bit of a tight fit in that hatch and all I could do when the bee went inside my clothes was to reach down with my jammy spoon and get him out. The fine fellow must have liked the jam, too, for he stayed on the spoon havin' a good feed from it. Then he cleaned himself up and flew off again—and mind you, we were two miles or more from the land then.'

'You didn't kill it, then?' David said superfluously.

'Not me, boy. I'd never kill a bee. I might want him to fertilise my roses for me some day.'

'You are planning to leave the sea eventually?' David felt the question might be cruel and added hastily, 'I mean, you intend to have a garden some time or other?'

'I'll have my garden right enough when I retire,' Zannah told him firmly. 'And there'll be nothin' in it but roses. That's all that's goin' to console me when I have to give up the sea. Just roses.' She was completely serious. 'The growers have been sendin' me catalogues for years now though I've never bought a bush from them. But the day will come when I'll be sendin' them orders for hundreds of roses.' Her eyes grew radiant. 'Me and old Mush there, when we take to the land we're goin' to have such a rose garden as folks will come for miles to see. Madam Butterfly; Shot Silk; Caroline Testout, and all the good old scented ones. I'll have to have scented roses to stop me gettin' the smell of the sea too strong,' she added. Her spread hand had been patting the table but with sudden decision she picked up her cup and drained the rest of the tea. 'Aye, and I'll not be content with roses just in the garden,' she went on. 'I'm goin' to have rose-patterned wall-paper and rose figured chintzes and roses on my china and anythin' else I can get with roses on it. I've been rose-starved all my life.' Her laughter started to bubble up again but she checked it to say, 'I was born in a slum, you know.'

'She'd grow roses on the boat if she could manage it,' said Spice.

'No, no.' Zannah was firm. 'Boats and roses don't mix.'

David quoted: ' "The mast burst open with a rose." '

'What's that?' demanded Zannah.

'It's a bit of a poem I once learned at school,' David said.

'How does it go?' It was Spice this time who asked the question.

'I can only remember the end of it now,' he confessed.

'Well, tell us that bit,' insisted Zannah.

> 'It was so old a ship, who knows, who knows?
> And yet so beautiful I watched in vain
> To see the mast burst open with a rose,
> And the whole deck put on its leaves again.'

Zannah said, '*Spizannah*'s not as old as all that but it's an idea, isn't it? Have her put ashore and set down in the middle of the bit of land I've chosen for my rose garden. We could go on living in her then.'

Spice looked straight into her aunt's eyes across the table. 'You couldn't do that to her,' she said.

'No,' said Zannah, and her voice was sad. 'No, I don't believe I could.'

The fo'c'sle was quiet for a few minutes except for the singing of the sea round the hull and the singing of the kettle on the stove. Spice jumped up.

'Time you were going, young man,' she commanded. 'Other people have work to do if you haven't.'

Zannah got up. 'I'll give you five minutes to say good night in the dry,' she said, and then turning to Spice adjured her: 'Just see he doesn't turn his head goin' up on deck.' She waddled off.

David slid his arms round Spice. 'Five minutes!' he said.

'It'll soon pass,' she teased and then her arms were around his neck and her mouth soft on his. She pushed him away.

off you go,' she said, urging him towards the steps, 'and 'don't look to your right as you go out of here.'

'Why ever not? Got a body stowed away or something?'

'In a manner of speaking, yes,' she replied.

'In a manner of speaking, how?'

'Nosy!'

'Close-mouth!'

'It's Aunt Zannah. She's on the lavatory and she's too fat to close the door so you have to go past without looking. Now then, are you satisfied? Off you go!'

All evening he had been wanting to talk of themselves and now, with the evening at an end, he found there had been no opportunity and that he knew almost nothing about Spice.

At the top of the steps he turned round. Spice stood blocking his view below.

'When can we meet again?'

'Next time we're in port together,' she replied.

'How soon will that be?'

'A fortnight today if everything goes to plan,' she said. 'Will you be here?'

'I should be,' he said. 'I'm going out with Noddy till the end of the season but we'll be back weekends.'

'If everything goes to plan,' she corrected. 'You can't be definite when you're earning your living from the sea.'

'All right,' he said. 'But if we're both here in a fortnight's time, promise you'll spend the evening with me, either at the dance or somewhere else?'

'Promise.'

'And you'll write me a letter ready for next weekend?' he pleaded. 'Send it care of the Post Office. I'll pick it up there.'

There was a noisy pumping below and Zannah's voice came up to him. 'It's time that hatch was closed, the rain's pelting in.'

'I'll write.' Spice urged him away. 'Good night, Dave,' she said, her voice soft and caressing.

'Good night,' he said reluctantly. The hatch closed. He climbed back to the pier and raced through the rain to *Fair Lassie*.

Chapter 12

He stayed with Noddy until the end of the lobster season, making the *Fair Lassie* his home until she went up on the slip for her annual overhaul. By then it was well into November and he was faced with the alternative of finding some sort of work to do around the port until the lobster season recommenced in the spring or if none were obtainable of packing his rucksack and going in search of a job elsewhere, in which case he would not be on hand to grasp the chance of a berth if and when one became available. Noddy had promised him that if he was still around and still keen to join him he could have Brad's berth on the *Fair Lassie*, Brad having returned to what was now expected to be a permanent berth on one of the herring boats. With such a promise David felt justified in looking for a cheap room and living on his small savings and the hope that he might hear of something in the way of a berth or a job that would tide him over the winter.

His weeks on the *Fair Lassie* had taught him much, not only about fishing and the men involved but also about himself. He recognised that his hankering for the life of a fisherman had now become in the nature of a passion. The inspiriting daily contest with the sea and the joyous revelation of his own strength when compelled to exert every muscle to its utmost limits were engendering in him a manhood which hitherto had been only a boyish dream. The tense expectancy which gripped him as he waited for the catch to break surface affected him like a gambler awaiting the spinning of the roulette wheel; the drama of watching a valiant boat fighting her battle against a challenging sea was as heart-swelling as watching a favourite runner break out from the ruck to win a close race. Every day brought its moments of ecstasy, even if it was only the seductive embrace of his bunk and the immediate engulfment by sleep. He liked the masculine austerity of the fo'c'sle; the matiness; the man-sized appetites and mammoth meals; the telling of Highland tales by Noddy in a soft and reverent voice. There were times of course when he had joined wholeheartedly with the rest of the crew when, after a brutish day had worn them to despair and exhaustion, they had chided themselves for not being content to stay on land. Like them he had cursed the sea with hysterical vehemence when it was in the ugliest and most treacherous moods but like them he knew that he was bewitched by it and that so long as body and mind remained fit enough he would never again be content with any other life.

He was also bewitched by Spice. That much he had to admit. Except when work was too exacting he found her face came between him and the task he was engaged on; when the hours permitted for sleep were abundant enough to allow dreams to percolate, his dreams were of Spice; his solitary meditations on deck at night were filled with plans for seeing her again. When there was a chance of *Spizannah* being in the harbour at weekends he was in a fever of impatience to get ashore and would go galloping up the pier in search of Spice the moment he was free; the few hours they managed together were spent in the rapt discovery of their own accord; their letters were full of love and yearning. But because of his obsession with the sea he found it easier to be ruthless with himself; easier to relegate Spice to the place of second mistress —a land love for weekends—distinct and apart from his daily life. He knew that if she showed jealousy or tried to wean him from his love of the sea it would in the final outcome be Spice who would find herself deserted.

It was unfortunate that David's predilection for the sea was not sufficient recommendation for skippers to be willing to try him out as a member of their crews at the winter herring-fishing. Noddy had said he would commend him as a strong, willing and amiable body to have aboard, but berths generally were much sought after and the skipper, unless he was despised as incapable, could usually take his pick from several experienced seamen. Eggo had mentioned a berth coming vacant on one of the boats only the previous weekend; 'She's called the *Virgin*,' he had explained and added with a wink, 'And she's the only virgin you're ever likely to come across in this port.'

Noddy had advised him not to bother to apply. 'You've got to be either a mason or a Roman Catholic to get on some of the boats,' he said, shaking his head, 'and that one's Catholic.'

Ignoring his advice David had gone to see the skipper who greeted him affably. He had asked if David was enjoying his 'fishing holiday'; had seemed surprised that he was still content to stay in the port, but not for one moment did he allow himself to entertain the idea that David's application for a berth was in any way serious. Disillusioned, David had returned to report to Noddy.

'Mixed crews don't mix,' Noddy commented enigmatically.

A week in the port with nothing to do but watch the boats coming and going had filled David with restlessness. He had applied for a job in the kipper factory and as a labourer on the pier, but all he had been given were vague promises, 'Maybe in a week or two—when the herrin's properly in.' Once or twice the idea of re-joining Donald had entered his mind. Donald was still convalescent but David felt he was capable of managing the *Silver Spray* himself with the older man there merely to act as a guide. He had even got as far as the telephone kiosk one day thinking that he would suggest this to Donald but, waiting by the kiosk, he had overheard one of the skippers excitedly shouting the details of his catch over the phone to some buyer. He had turned away, realising finally that he had outgrown the almost frivolous small boat fishing of those days on the *Silver Spray* and that if he forsook the precincts of the port now his chances of ever becoming a real fisherman would be jeopardised. Someday, perhaps, he promised himself, when he was more affluent, he might treat himself to a busman's holiday with Donald, but just now fishing was too serious a business.

He went up to the Post Office to collect the letter Spice always contrived to post to him so that he received it on a Saturday. His spirits sank to a lower level of gloom as, reading it through quickly, he found there was no likelihood of the *Spizannah* being in port for at least another month. He returned to the pier to try to find comfort among the presence of boats he might some time be lucky enough to work on. Hearing his name called he looked up and saw Brad sauntering towards him. Brad's flat face was enlivened by the prospect of good earnings but he was considerate enough to greet David with concern for his circumstances.

'Still wantin' a berth, Beardie?' he asked.

'You know that without asking,' David retorted.

Brad looked over his shoulder and though there was no one within earshot except the ubiquitous Saturday urchins, he spoke through the side of his mouth.

'You could try our own skipper,' he confided.

'What, "King Herring"? Is it likely?' David's spirits which had soared temporarily sank to a lower level of gloom, as he recalled the big man he had encountered in the bar on the day of his arrival and who had been responsible for dubbing him 'Beardie'.

'Why not? There's talk that one of the crew's got somethin' wrong with his stomach and has to go to hospital with it. I've only just heard myself so I slipped down to give you the word.'

David was suitably thankful but the possibility of the acknowledged king of skippers allowing a greenhorn like himself to join his crew was too remote to warrant more than a moment's optimism.

'He can take his pick from the whole port,' he pointed out.

'Aye, right enough. But the only two men short of berths just now are both Roman Catholics and he doesn't like the smell of 'em much.' Brad took out two cigarettes and handed one to David. 'It's worth a try, Beardie. I know Big Cam doesn't mislike your face and he can only say "no".'

David, remembering the forcefulness of the man, suspected that he would say a lot more than 'no', but Brad sounded so earnest that he had to promise he would at least try.

'Go up to the pub a bit on the early side tonight and see will you catch himself while he's fairly sober,' Brad suggested.

'How early?' asked David, prepared to go there and then if it would satisfy him.

Brad took a brand new watch from his pocket. 'Ach, we've not been in more than a couple of hours. He won't have finished with his wife yet.' He winked. 'So, say in another three hours' time and you may be lucky.'

David thanked him, and, conscious of a slight lessening of the day's gloom agreed to Brad's suggestion that they should go to the tea-room, forbearing to express his surprise that it was not to be the pub.

'There's one thing you must keep in mind, though,' Brad cautioned as they walked along. ' "King Herring's" not like Noddy. No, by God! He's a damned hard skipper. He works his men like bloody blacks and if you get with him there's no job he won't expect you to tackle. There's only one thing he won't do though, and that's expect you to work harder than he works himself.'

'I'll work, given the chance,' David said grimly.

'So long as you know,' said Brad.

They reached the tea-room and the reason for Brad's suggesting it was immediately obvious. The tables were thronged with kipper girls and their predatory enticements were the solace Brad needed after his week of celibacy. His expression became ecstatic; his eyes, under half-closed lids, roved speculatively over them as he prepared for conquest.

At first David retaliated easily to their taunts and insinuating laughter but as the repartee grew more and more unrestrained he felt the back of his neck growing hot and fled in sheer terror of their voracity. He decided he wanted to re-read his letter from Spice and with this intention returned to his lodging.

He had been lucky enough to get lodgings at a rent he could afford in the village with an old lady who liked to keep a couple of lodgers more for company than from any motive of profit-making. Her house was homely and she herself was cheerful and preferred to err on the side of overfeeding her lodgers than otherwise. In her cosy, fire-bright kitchen she would set David's piled plate on the table, watch him until he had finished and press him to take more. When he firmly refused she would lift the big brown teapot from the hob and pour tea into his cup until both cup and saucer were overflowing and he had to shout 'Whoa' before she would desist. He discovered later that her eyesight was so poor she could only just make out the vague shapes of the utensils and rather than risk being thought mean she continued to dispense food and drink until she could detect a note of panic in the recipient's voice.

Back in his bedroom he read Spice's letter and lying on his bed allowed himself to ponder Brad's suggestion. A berth on the 'King's' boat! Would he stand a chance? If he did, David thought, it would indeed be like 'hobnobbing with the nobility'.

He stifled any thrusts of optimism so resolutely that when he eventually reached the pub and even after he had imbibed what was supposed to be a fortifying dram and a half pint he had rejected the possibility altogether. By the time Big Cam put in an appearance he had so defeated hope that he could only nod to him perfunctorily before turning back to his drink.

A moment later his shoulder was in the grip of a large hand.

'Hullo there, Beardie! Just the man I was thinkin' I might see.' David turned to him with a wary smile and saw the heavily handsome face was full of cordiality. Big Cam called for drinks. 'They tell me you're lookin' for a berth,' he said, leaning his folded arms on the counter and looking at David through narrowed eyes.

'That's right,' David confessed. 'Heard of anything that might suit me?'

'You're mighty keen on the fishin', then?' he asked.

'Dead keen,' rejoined David.

'Take your drink,' Big Cam said and tossed his own off at a gulp. Without command the barman produced another one for him. David felt hope prickling against the back of his mind as Big Cam resumed: 'Matter of fact, I'm short of a crew myself. One of my bastards has got to go into hospital.'

'Any chance for me?' asked David boldly. He waited, dreading a rebuff, while the big man tossed off another dram.

'You're a bit of a "green hand", but I'll give you a try for a week if you want it.' The reply was offhand and after he had spoken he turned his frost-blue gaze on the half-listening drinkers around them.

Looking straight at him, David said, 'I want it.'

'Okay then, that's settled. Mind you, I wouldn't have even offered you the chance only for Noddy tellin' me you're a good worker.'

'I'll buy him a drink for that,' David said with a smile.

'See that you do that,' said Big Cam and went on. 'Aye, well now. I'll see you Monday mornin' down at the boat.' He banged down his glass and made to go. 'I haven't rightly started my night's drinkin' yet,' he excused himself, 'for I've promised to take the wife up to see her sister for an hour or two. I'll be comin' back after that.' Halfway out he turned and came back to David.

'There's just one thing I want to warn you of, Beardie,' he said with a touch of aggressiveness. 'It's well known I work my crews hard—you've heard that?'

David nodded.

'And I'll call you all the bloody names I can lay my tongue to but you'll not take too much notice of me, for I don't mean it half the time.'

David smiled. 'What about the other half?' he asked.

Big Cam grabbed a fistful of David's jersey. 'You'll bloody well find out I mean every word I say,' he threatened. He released his hold, called a light-hearted 'Cheerio' and shouldered his way out.

David turned to find Brad beside him.

'So you're on?' Brad was obviously pleased.

'I am—if he doesn't change his mind by Monday,' said David, still afraid to accept his good fortune.

'He'll not change. You always know where you are with the "King".'

Chapter 13

Soon after eight o'clock on Monday morning *Silver Huntress* in company with her 'neebor' boat *Silver Venture*, was steaming out of the harbour towards a white-crested sea with David the only visibly elated member of an otherwise morose crew. In addition to David and the skipper there were Brad; Chick, the cook; Josh, the boy; Alex, the veteran of them all, and Fergy, the skipper's second-in-command. Chick was gangling, hollow-cheeked and bulbous-eyed. Josh was snub-nosed and chubby-faced with eyes like spoonfuls of golden syrup and of a softness that somehow belied his reputation of being 'wild, but not all bad'. Brad said that he had been at one time the most blasphemous boy in the port but that since he had taken a great fancy to a devoutly religious girl his language had moderated considerably. Hearing him sometimes David doubted if the latter part of the report could be true.

Alex was plump with white hair and eyes that had grown tranquil with long staring into distance. His trim black brows looked as if they were brushed regularly with boot polish and under a semi-permanent mist of grey his cheeks had the freshness of a youth's. Fergy was of medium height and compact, with eyes of a cold metallic blue and a head of close-cropped fair hair that made him look as if he was wearing a skull-cap made of dressed tripe. His face was tight-drawn; his lips rarely relaxed from a thin vexed line. He exuded irascibility and from the moment he stepped aboard David was aware that for some reason Fergy had made up his mind to detest him.

Big Cam who, though his large bulk was slouched in a half-comatose position in the wheelhouse yet whose alert eyes would have undoubtedly discerned a fly landing on the deck of his boat, called David.

'Fergy'll likely not take to you for a whiley,' he explained confidentially. 'He was badly wantin' that berth for a relative of his, though God knows why. Fergy either can't or won't see it but the man's only a thunderin' great slob that's under his wife's thumb every minute he's ashore. He's not much better when he's at sea either, for when there comes a bit of a blow the fellow's down on his knees prayin' to the Lord not to make his poor, dear wife a widow. He fairly gives a man the creeps.'

David's mouth twisted into a dubious smile.

'It's as true as I'm here,' affirmed the skipper. 'The bastard's not such a bad worker when he's not tired out but there's times at the beginning of the week when you'll hardly get more than a flicker of life out of him.'

'His wife?' queried David with a suggestive laugh.

'Aye, his wife in a manner of speakin'. But not what you're thinkin', you dirty-minded lout.' The skipper's disgust was well simulated, David thought. 'He gets no sleep because his wife's a tartar for takin' in tourists in the season and she likes their money so much she canna bear to turn any of them away. When the man gets home from the sea he'll find as likely as not she's let his bed to the tourists and he's nowhere to sleep.'

'You'd think he'd put his foot down,' murmured David inattentively. He was staring at the vapour trail of a plane that could have been a reflection of their own course.

'He needs to do more than put his foot down,' the skipper advocated, 'he needs to take his belt to her.' David smiled inwardly. The big man's own slip of a wife adored him and his attitude to her was all gentleness and banter. 'Why,' the skipper continued, 'I've known the poor man wanderin' around the place all hours of the night waitin' for the visitors to go to bed so that he can make himself a bed in the bath-room—supposin' she's not let that, too.' He snorted. 'I'm tellin' you, Beardie, that's greed, not need.'

'Why doesn't he bunk on one of the boats?' David asked.

'She won't have him do that. No, no, the neighbours isn't supposed to know what she's up to. She thinks she has them all fooled.'

Soon after the boat had reached open water Chick came up to tell them their tea was ready and calling Brad to take the helm the skipper went below. David followed. Alex, Josh and Fergy were already cutting slices of butter from the block on the table and laying them between warm rolls, which the local baker, as a concession to departing fishermen, supplied especially early on Monday mornings. This pre-breakfast snack was now an established custom and, David suspected, played its part in assuaging the pangs of leave-taking and combating the langours of the weekend hangover.

David was about to take his first mouthful of roll when his 'toorie' cap was snatched roughly from his head and thrown on the bunk beside him. With his mouth still open he spun round in surprise to find Fergy glaring at him.

'That's the first thing you can learn on this boat!' Fergy snarled. 'No man sits down to a meal here with a cap on.'

'Okay, okay. Take it easy,' David said, forcing himself to remain calm.

'I know a boat where you'd have been told by a swipe across the face first,' the skipper confirmed between sucks of tea.

'Aye, and that's what he'll get from me if he needs a second tellin',' threatened Fergy.

David stuffed his mouth full of roll to choke back the

retort that rose to his lips. If there was a rule, no matter how incomprehensible it might be, he would observe it. But he wished he had found out about it without giving Fergy the chance to be unpleasant. He wondered what prompted these men who were prepared to go to a dance unshaved and un-changed to solemnly remove their hats before sitting down to eat what was not even considered to be more than 'a bite to see us on'.

When Fergy had gone aft he turned to Alex. 'This business of taking off your hat before eating—is it a superstition?' he asked quietly.

The skipper put down his paper to say forcefully: 'No, it's not superstition, it's manners.'

David shook his head in bewilderment. 'Noddy used to say grace before meals,' he told them, 'but he didn't bother to take his hat off to do it.'

'Noddy has as many manners as a frog has feathers,' re-torted the skipper and, snatching a James Bond from under the nose of the startled Josh, retired with it to his bunk.

Alex explained. 'I daresay in the days when bein' a fisher-man meant half starvin', folks was that grateful for food they'd be after thankin' God for every bite. I daresay that's when all this hat takin'-off started. It's not so long ago as all that, either,' he added meditatively.

'D'you remember those days?' David liked to get the older fishermen reminiscing.

'Aye, a bit of them.' He filled his pipe before he went on. 'You got your plate of food on the days you were lucky and you'd spend a long time lookin' at it wonderin' if you could afford to eat it or whether it wasn't best saved until your belly got even emptier.' He sat back, puffing contentedly. 'Things is a lot different now but some of us went pretty hungry then.'

'And look at the shape of him now,' said Chick, who had just been released from watch. 'Don't you believe a word he says, Beardie. That stomach of his has never grumbled about anythin' except that it was too full.'

Alex let a smile flit over his face and made no comment. Chick stoked up the stove and busied himself with the preparations for breakfast. Alex held his head in his hands, his elbows resting on the table, his eyes closed. Josh had found another paperback and was lying in his bunk reading it. The fo'c'sle grew stuffy.

'You'd best go and let Fergy come for his breakfast,' Chick said to David. 'You might just as well keep watch with Brad as anybody else.'

There was so much to learn: David found out how much when he joined Brad in the wheelhouse and was told something of the work he would be expected to do once they got among the herring. David would be put on the 'corks', Brad explained, which meant that he would have to haul the rope along the top of the net. It was hard work but not as hard as Brad's own more skilled job of dealing with the sole ropes.

'Until the soles are up there's a gap in the net,' Brad told him. 'You canna afford to have that.'

He proceeded to give David a résumé of events as they would probably happen. As soon as they had taken their dinner, he said, they would be off with their 'neebor' to look for signs of shoals with the aid of their echo-sounders.

'How long before you usually find anything?' David asked.

'Depends,' said Brad non-committally. 'If we're lucky maybe only two or three hours. Other times you can search till eight or nine o'clock in the mornin' and still not find sight nor sound of the beasties. That means eighteen hours or more on deck for us with only a wee spell in the fo'c'sle while you unfreeze yourself with a smoke and a cup of tea.' Brad sucked in his breath. 'It's pretty tough when it's like that,' he said. 'Of course, that's with our skipper. Some of the other skippers wouldn't bother to go on so long. If they haven't found a shoal by three or four o'clock in the mornin' they give up and go and anchor while they have a kip.'

He shook his head. 'It wouldn't do for Big Cam, that.'

'All right so far,' David said. 'Now what happens when we do find a shoal?'

'Then the swearin' and shoutin' starts,' said Brad with a short bark of laughter. 'You'll have to shift yourself then, Beardie. You'll work till the sweat's runnin' down into your boots and your guts feels as if they're goin' to burst through your trousers, but you daren't stop. The skipper's thrown a man overboard before now for slackin'.'

David looked at him askance.

'Aye, he did right enough. Mind you, he fished him out again afterwards but he told him if it happened again he wouldn't bother.' Brad frowned. 'Aye, like I told you, he's the finest skipper hereabouts but he's a bloody villain when he's fishin'. Not that you can blame him,' he added. 'There's too much risk of things goin' wrong when you're at the herrin'.'

'Such as?' David was anxious to avoid the risk of being thrown into that wintry sea.

'Well, you might get a net full of coral that'll tear it to pieces in no time. Or maybe the net starts to roll up—there's always the danger of that and believe me it's a right bugger of a mess when it happens. The thing you have to watch with herrin' is that once it's dried up—dried up means it's all in the net and alongside the boat—you've got to work fast, real fast. If a boat's slow gettin' the fish out then more than half of it's goin' to be dead and if there's too many of the herrin' dead then your net's goin' to burst.'

David was trying to understand but he was still a good deal perplexed. Why, he asked himself, should the net burst with a load of dead herring and yet not with a load of live herring? His mind, worrying at the problem, came up with the solution as Brad continued.

'While the herrin's alive it's still swimmin', see?' he explained with great patience. 'And in its fright, thank God, it doesn't all swim the same way at the same time. Not as a rule, anyway. Mind you,' he emphasised, 'I've seen that happen before now. I mind one night we had the herring almost dried up and suddenly somethin' triggered them off and they just turned and took charge of everythin'. Swam off with the net and the corks, aye, and the cook as well they took with them. We lost the bloody lot and we reckoned it was about a hundred and fifty cran in all.' Brad glanced to see how impressed David was. 'It was like as though those herrin' was playin' a game of "follow my leader" and by God! they had a damn good leader.'

'What about the cook?' David asked.

'Oh, we got him out, the clumsy bastard.'

'There's one more thing I'd like to know,' said David as Chick's head bobbed up and Fergy reappeared to take over the wheel. 'Am I supposed to do anything else apart from hauling on these corks?'

'That depends,' Brad replied. 'The best thing is to keep your ears and eyes skinned and jump to it the minute you're told to do anythin'. Remember to do that and to keep out of everybody else's way at the same time and you'll be okay.'

They went down to the fo'c'sle. It was only an hour since they had stuffed themselves with tea and rolls and now they were ready to stuff themselves with sausages and bacon and eggs. The life at sea allied to the proximity of the galley chimney, whose smoke enwrapped them continuously in hunger-making smells, was a constant spur to the appetite. When one o'clock came round David's mouth was already watering at the prospect of a good plate of the stew and dumplings he had seen Chick cooking.

'Do you ever eat any of the herring you catch?' he asked Brad.

'Aye, Chick'll always do you a fry if you fancy it.'

After they had listened to the shipping forecast the radio was left on for 'Listen with Mother', during which programme neither Fergy nor Chick would tolerate any trivial interruption.

'It's nice to think of the little buggers enjoyin' themselves,' Chick gave as the explanation.

Replete, oilskin-shrouded and resolved for hard work they went up on deck to keep watch while the *Silver Huntress* quested the sea for shoals. In the wheelhouse the echo-sounder ticked away while over the ship to ship radio the skipper called question and answer to their similarly occupied neighbour, *Silver Venture*.

The *Silver Huntress* was a bigger, more modern boat than the *Fair Lassie* and boasted many more refinements. The fo'c'sle had more headroom and the bunks were roomier, though not much; the lockers were padded; the galley was resplendent with stainless steel and modern plastics and instead of the 'bucket and rope' she had a properly fitted pump-operated toilet—'a lavatory with a handbrake on it' was how Brad described it. The fo'c'sle floor was covered with coir matting which Chick took up every day and which he dipped in the sea every weekend. There was coir matting also in the wheelhouse but this was fastened down by metal beer bottle caps in a pattern of colours that had obviously been contrived and executed with much care. David thought it likely that the crew had been under orders as to which brands of beer they must drink in order to provide the requisite caps. So far as David was concerned there was another big advantage the boat had over the *Fair Lassie* and that was her easier motion. In the design of fishing boats there is, or should be—so he had learned from his avid reading of various fishing and boating weeklies he had come across—a factor taken into consideration which is known as 'sea-kindliness' and relates to the effect of a boat's motion upon her crew. *Fair Lassie* was indubitably a splendidly sea-worthy boat but she was hard on her crew in that she flung herself about so much in bad weather the crew became exhausted as much from the sheer physical effort of keeping their balance as from the actual labour of fishing. The *Silver Huntress* on the other hand was perhaps less submissive to a savage sea and as consequence her motion was far less demanding on her crew. She was illustrating her superiority now in riding the choppy seas with sinuous ease.

The day was beginning to fade; the sky darkening slowly with something of a 'pointillism' effect; the cold had become sharp-edged, causing the crew to sporadically flap their arms and stamp their feet; the pallid gleams of lighthouses strengthened to brightness, night mushroomed over them and still the boat searched on. Three hours had gone by when suddenly there was a shout from the skipper and immediately the boat turned.

'Standby!'

'Sounds like it,' said Brad, pushing past David.

'Way Winky!' The buoy with its flashing light went over and the net was shot as they steamed in a wide semicircle. Their masthead light flashed the message to their neighbour to close the net, and soon the *Silver Venture* touched fenders briefly to put some of her crew aboard before taking the *Silver Huntress* and towing her beam-on away from the net. The two boats worked as a team but that did not stop the two skippers from waging constant and acrimonious war with each other. Back and fro through the turmoil of the hauling their condemnation of each other crackled.

'What the hell's that bastard doin'? Stop shovin' your stern out, you bugger!'

'Easy there, blast you!'

'Easy yourself, you bastard!'

The noise of the herring, trapped and struggling in the net, came to David's ears like the urgent sound of water coming to the boil. He stared at the water, becoming aware of the presence of other boats making intricate manœuvres as they tried to pick up part of the shoal. Their own net appeared to be full of fish; the air was splintered with recriminations; the crew dashed about and worked frenziedly but not fast enough to satisfy 'King Herring'.

'Come on, you lazy fat slobs! Haul, will you! Use some of them sausages you had for your breakfast! What the hell d'you think you're fed like cocks for if it's not to work? Come on, haul! Haul! Damn you. Haul!'

They sweated and strained at the ropes as the winch rumbled on.

'Soles up! Go easy on them corks, there!' David went easy. The skipper danced to and from the wheelhouse, helping and instructing between hurling invective at the other boat.

'Okay! Lights on!'

The soles were up, the bag of the net was tight so that no more herring could escape, but there was no respite for the men. Left like that too big a proportion of the herring would be suffocated. The net had to be emptied quickly. The hooped net of the brailer went down again and again, lifting and pouring its quivering silver loads into the hold of the *Silver Huntress*. The net was taken aboard, overhauled and shot again, going through the same procedure, but still the skipper was not satisfied with the catch. The crew had been fifteen hours on deck without a break and were panting and puffing as the net went out for the third time.

'Oh, for a smoke!' said Brad, gingerly straightening his back for a moment. But there was no time to grope for a cigarette and light it.

'Smoke, is it, boys? You want a smoke, do you?' The skipper had overheard Brad's remark and taking five cigarettes from a packet in the wheelhouse he stuck them all in his mouth and lit them. The crew waited, yearning for the moment he would push one between their eager lips, but instead he continued to puff at them himself. When their expressions were sufficiently aghast he took out all five cigarettes and flung them into the sea.

'That'll teach you to work when you're told to,' he taunted. Bitterness and disappointment engulfed the crew and they murmured among themselves. 'I'm here to make this boat pay and I'll make it pay if I have to put a crew of bloody blacks aboard!' he yelled at them.

'If you put a crew of blacks aboard they'd cut your throat for you in half an hour,' Fergy retorted, expressing the savagery they all felt at that moment.

The hold was full of herring after the third haul and they wedged it in with fish boxes or spars of wood—anything that would stop the fish sliding about and rubbing off its bright scales so that it would lose its market value. They were ready then to steam off to market with it while their neighbour was left to explore the sea for prospects for the next night's fishing. The men relaxed. David looked at their tired faces, caked with salt and spattered with herring scales.

'Any shoppin' you want doin', neebour?' The skipper's now affable voice enquired over the radio. After a moment's listening he called for Chick. 'He's wantin' more sugar and bacon and a packet of cornflakes. Got it?'

Chick nodded and disappeared below.

'Okay, boys, you can go and get your heads down for an hour. Alex can stay and keep watch with me up here.' It was, David noticed, the older men who seemed to be able to do without sleep more easily. Down below the crew drank hot mugs of tea and ate more bread and jam before tumbling into their bunks to abandon themselves to the luxury of an hour's sleep until they would be called for the work of unloading.

The *Silver Huntress* foamed aggressively into the harbour to be greeted by the inevitable gulls, brisk fish salesmen and impatient buyers. The noise of the clanging fish bell came above the throb of engines, the revving of lorries and all the bustle and confusion of unloading. Brad and David stood among the herring in the hold, shovelling it into the basket which the derrick swung above the waiting lorry. Alex guided the basket to tip its load into the piled boxes while Josh spread them with shovelfuls of granulated ice. The skipper and Fergy were standing some distance away having what they called a 'wee crack' with one of their colleagues and there was no knowing from their poker-faced expressions whether or not their herring had brought a good price. Chick, who had been up to the village to do his shopping, returned looking pleased. He nodded towards the hold and winked. Brad and David resumed their shovelling with increased zest.

The hold was empty at last. They hosed it down, hosed the decks and hosed the slime and fish scales from each other's oilskins. The skipper and Fergy returned and they were off to sea again, ready to contact the *Silver Venture* and begin another night's fishing.

Chapter 14

The herring continued to shoal in quantities that satisfied the crew if not the skipper. The men began to look smug and to wear what were described locally as their 'herring faces'. On calm Friday nights when the laden boats were steaming home for the weekend the crews would join in an impromptu sing-song: during a lull in the conversation a voice humming a Gaelic song would drift over the boat's radio; a more confident voice would take up the tune, a mouth-organ would begin an exuberant accompaniment and soon all the crews of all the boats were singing, letting their voices soar above the urgent thudding of the engines. The port, made busy by the increasing number of boats bringing in their catches, braced itself to deal with the silver harvest; the kipper factory worked overtime smoking the silver into gold; the wives of the crews planned the refurbishing of their homes.

Christmas was drawing near and David was now accepted as a competent member of the crew of the *Silver Huntress*. Occasionally he enquired with a not entirely spurious concern after the health of the man for whom he was deputising and it was with a guilty feeling of elation that he heard it would be at least another month before the man was fit again. With any luck, David thought, he might be able to hang on to his job until the end of the herring season came in February. A couple of weeks holiday then aboard the *Spizannah* would see him through until Noddy was ready to start once again on the lobsters. He cringed from the thought of being even temporarily without a berth; of being excluded from the rush and excitement of fishing; of not sharing the bawdy raillery and rank sentimentality of the fo'c'sle; of being left on the pier while the boats speared their way to the sea.

He also dreaded the loss of his wage packet. Already he had saved up enough to see him through the rest of the winter; enough to buy Christmas presents for Spice and Megan, but now he had the idea of getting hold of a motor-cycle again so that at weekends he could rush off to whichever port *Spizannah* happened to be lying. Now that winter had come Zannah had limited herself to cargoes that did not take her too far from her home port and consequently Spice and he were unable to meet as often as they would have liked. Being by this time very much in love he had lost all desire to attend the Saturday-night dances which were the only entertainment apart from the pub which the port offered and as a result his weekends ashore were divided into periods of sleeping, writing long letters to Spice that filled him with a restless yearning and of drinking good money away at the pub in order to counteract the yearning. To his sister Megan he wrote less often, to his parents not at all. Megan wrote regularly and her letters reiterated her happiness. She had reported that her mother had visited her twice of late, both times when her father was busy at the shop. She thought their attitude to Harry was gradually softening, particularly since she had persuaded him to attend chapel with her occasionally. She was hoping, she wrote, that they would relent sufficiently to come to tea with her sometime during the Christmas holiday. Regarding their attitude to David, she saw no signs yet of any yielding in their determination to disavow him, but he was not to worry, she pleaded, she was sure they would forgive him eventually. She had added a postcript in her last letter suggesting he sent them a Christmas card just to show he harboured no bitterness towards them. Bitterness? David realised with a shock that except for the night *Fair Lassie* had been on the rock he had hardly given his parents a thought, bitter or otherwise.

At the beginning of Christmas week the crew of the *Silver Huntress*, like the crews of all the other boats in the port, were becoming increasingly high-spirited as they looked forward to New Year, when the port would be closed for a whole week and they could forsake fishing and abandon themselves to their annual orgy. David too was elated, but only because he would soon be seeing Spice again, Zannah having invited him to spend Christmas with them aboard the *Spizannah*.

On this particular Monday there was an additional reason for levity aboard the *Silver Huntress* for on the preceding Saturday Alex had astounded everyone by secretly going off to a registrar's office and getting himself married. Bride and groom had gone to the pictures for their honeymoon and had then returned home in a taxi, well laden with bottles, and announced their intention of having a reception to which the whole port was invited.

'Oh God, you should have been there,' Chick confided to David, who had missed the revelry because a bout of toothache had sent him to an early bed. 'We fairly made a night of it. Christ! You should have seen the goings-on.' He dipped his false teeth into the kettle of water that was to make their tea and fitted them back into his mouth. 'I got pissed as a newt,' he confessed.

Brad and Josh came aboard at that moment. 'I was just tellin' Beardie here he should have been at the party. It was a fair do, wasn't it, Brad?'

'I didn't stay long enough to find out,' said Brad tersely.

'You missed somethin', then!' expostulated Chick. 'It was a damty good party. The best I've ever been to in these parts. Lots of drinks.'

'Oh, aye, I saw there was plenty of drink,' Brad agreed.

'But I had all I could take before I got there, anyway.'

'What time did you come?' asked Chick solicitously.

'At the back of two,' Brad replied. 'I was feelin' fine, too. Thought I was fairly goin' to enjoy myself,' he went on lugubriously, 'but when I opened the door what did I see but that Bessie dancin' in the middle of the floor and with no clothes on.' He saw David's look of astonishment. 'Aye,' he affirmed, 'dancin' she was, with those bloody great paps of hers jiggin' up and down. My God! It was horrible. I just shut the door and came straight out again before I spewed up all my good whisky. You can keep them sort of parties.'

Chick grunted satirically. 'I never expected to hear you complainin' at a woman takin' her clothes off,' he exclaimed.

'Ach, hell, man. There's women and women,' Brad declared. 'And there's some jobs a man likes to do for himself, anyway.'

'You're a bloody perfectionist, you are,' grumbled Chick. Josh, who had been listening wide-eyed, chuckled appreciatively.

Alex, usually the first of the crew aboard on a Monday morning, was late and Big Cam was growing impatient.

'Ach, I expect he's forgotten how to put his trousers on,' Brad put forward as the excuse.

The engine was throbbing and all but the last rope was aboard when Alex came in sight. Supremely indifferent to the shouted ribaldry that came from the crews of nearby boats and also to the grinning faces of his companions on the *Silver Huntress*, Alex stepped aboard giving them only his customary nod of greeting. Down in the fo'c'sle he stowed his things as usual in his bunk and as usual took out his pipe and prepared to light up.

It was too much for Chick, who stared at him incredulously. 'Look at that!' he exploded. 'Married on Saturday and here today as if he's done nothin' with his arse all weekend except sit on it.'

'What else would I have done?' asked Alex innocently.

'Listen to him!' Chuck shouted. Alex's smile was un-ruffled.

'I don't believe he knows what to do,' Brad said with a show of astonishment, and his taunt was taken up gleefully by Josh and Chick.

'Is that the way of it, Alex? You don't know what's expected of you?' they demanded.

Alex quelled them with a bland smile. Taking the pipe from his mouth he said tolerantly:

'Maybe not, boys, but I daresay I'll find out when I need to.'

Later, in the wheelhouse, David asked Big Cam: 'How long has Alex known this woman he's married?'

'I don't know how long he's known her but he's been courtin' her for thirty years.'

'I would have thought he'd got past the marrying age by now,' David commented.

'Not at all,' repudiated the skipper. 'He's waited a bit longer than most folks maybe but he's young enough to marry. He's no more than sixty or thereabouts.'

'I think I'd like to settle down before then,' said David. 'By the time I'm thirty, I think.'

'That's gey young for a man to tie himself down,' Big Cam told him.

David went forward. It was an afternoon of perfect winter calm and he was able to walk nonchalantly along the steady deck. The hills were white-cloaked and positively etched against a sky that was a rippling blue and gold. The sea was a translucent turquoise, knobbed with black guillemots and white gulls. A window in an island cottage caught a shaft of the setting sun and burned with a bright, reflective glow. It seemed to David that everything was touched with lustre; the boat deck, the pile of floats, even the smoke from the galley chimney. He was convinced that these northern parts of

Britain enjoyed an exclusive quality of light. It was as if the spirit of the day so cherished the glory of the landscape that it reserved for it only the quintessence of its light. The cottage window lost its glow and receded into anonymity. David went back to the wheelhouse, where Big Cam was listening to the ship to ship radio.

The conversation struck David as being unusually refined. With puzzled enquiry he looked at the skipper. Big Cam chuckled.

'There's been another warnin' from the radio station on the mainland. Every now and then they threaten to report us for usin' bad language over the air. Nobody wants to see their names in the papers for swearin' so we have to try and remember to clean it up for a whiley.'

In this instance the warning appeared to have been a particularly effective one for in the middle of a staid description of the day's activities one of the skippers let out a loud and fulsome belch. Immediately there followed an anxious 'Pardon me—bad stomach'.

When the rest of the crew came up David went below to take a last mug of tea before donning his oilskins in readiness for work. The teapot was empty.

'I'll make do with tinker's tea,' David said, but Chick, ignoring him, brewed up another seven or eight pints in the big pot. He handed mugs up to the men on deck.

'How much ruddy tea d'you get through on this boat, Chick?' David asked.

'I reckon about twelve pounds in the week,' Chick said, opening the store-cupboard to show David his reserve stock of twenty-eight half-pound packets. 'That's just in case we get stuck anywhere,' he said.

David had intended to take his time over his tea for work would begin soon enough, but before he had swallowed more than a couple of mouthfuls there came a shout from the deck. Simultaneously empty tea mugs were being pushed through the hatch to Chick. David hurried into his smock and went up on deck.

The sea was silvery, lit by a thick slice of moon and a sprinkling of early stars. The crew were murmuring excitedly.

'Big shoal?' exclaimed Josh gloatingly.

The 'winky' light went over. 'Oh, lead, kindly bloody light!' Josh sang out. The neighbour boat was given the signal.

'By God! Look at it: So bloody thick you could walk on it!'

The crew summoned their strength for all-out effort.

'Watch out, there!'

'By God, it's wild! It's wild herrin'!'

'It's makin' inshore!' There was anguish in the voice.

'For Christ's sake, bang on the anchor!'

'Bang the anchor!' The command was taken up by every man on board and there began a concerted banging and thumping on anything that would produce a din so as to startle and confuse the fish.

'Searchlights on! Get your searchlights on, you blasted slobs. Are you deaf over there?' That was the skipper's voice shouting to the skipper of the *Silver Venture*. Amidst a spate of malediction the two boats like collies penning a flock of sheep drove the herring between them, at the same time flashing their lights on the shore to frighten the fish and make it turn back into the net. The shoal turned and, as the boats closed, commenced its terror-crazed leaping. The urgent murmur of the water was intensified by the immense size of the shoal and David held his breath in amazement as the fish came pouring over the corks in a solid scintillating river of green. The sight was hypnotic; it was inconceivable that such a vast number of fish could be contained in such a relatively small area of sea.

'Corks! Corks!' The skipper's vehement reprimand snapped David's attention back to his own task.

When the soles were up at last the net was near to bursting

with the amount of fish and there was a frenzied rush by both boats to get it emptied. The holds of both boats were full before the net came aboard. The crews gasped their congratulations to one another.

The skipper offered round a packet of cigarettes. 'Three hundred cran between us, I reckon,' he told them, 'and I reckon we lost another six hundred cran.'

'Aye, but they were wild,' commiserated Alex.

It was fortunate that the morning was calm, for the boats had a bare eighteen inches of freeboard, so heavy was their night's plunder.

'You'd best get them fenders in,' the skipper instructed. 'They'll be draggin', else.'

Down in the fo'c'sle the crew did some calculations. Three hundred cran—that was about forty-five tons of fish between the two boats. If the price was still good . . .?

Chick handed round mugs of tea. 'We've made a damty good Christmas present for ourselves out of it,' he observed happily.

Chapter 15

It was Christmas Eve and with a pocket full of money and a heart singing with anticipation, David was on his way to Glasgow in the back of a car belonging to one of his fishermen friends who was taking his wife and two of her relatives to shop at 'the barras' there. The car was small and the two women between whom he was wedged were substantial. They were also decidedly hilarious and when their bodies quaked with frequent laughter his own had perforce to quake in harmony.

'They're lovely, the barras,' the women assured David. 'That's where you should go to do your shopping. What you can't get there for half a crown isn't worth mentioning.'

From their description he judged the 'barras' to be some sort of street market and at first it struck him as odd that the prospect should not only warrant such a long journey but should generate so much excitement. However when he reflected on the limited merchandise offered by the few drab and uncompetitive shops of the port he began to appreciate that in contrast the flashy stalls would indeed represent a veritable wonderland of colour and bargain hunting. He did not accompany them to the 'barras' but instead turned his steps to Sauchiehall Street where he bought for Spice the thickest, gayest woollen sweater he could find and ordered another, not quite so flamboyant, to be sent to Megan. The sweaters were his own idea and were bought simply because within the range of garments he was confident enough to shop for on his own he considered there was nothing to compare with them for making a woman look delectable and cuddly. For Mush he had already acquired a bottle of the 'wild stuff' and for Zannah he had been lucky enough to find an illustrated book on roses. Satisfied, and with his rucksack bulging, he caught a train to the port where he would find the *Spizannah* lying.

It was late when he arrived but Spice was there to meet him. He pulled her into the dim waiting room where they clung to each other ecstatically until an impatient porter, anxious to lock up for the night, routed them out. Arm in arm, with love and delight in each other providing an armour against the frost-sharpened wind and flurries of sleet that assaulted them each time they turned a corner, they made their way to the pier. The *Spizannah* lay tranquil at the quayside, her lighted portholes beaming a welcome; it was wonderful to step aboard again, wonderful to go down into that friendly cabin and have Zannah greet him as if he were Santa Claus himself while Mush shook his hand so vigorously that his cap fell off. There was immediately a dram to be swallowed to the accompaniment of enthusiastic '*Slainte Mhaths*'; there was supper to be eaten and experiences to be exchanged. A final dram to a toast of 'Lang may your lum reek' was followed by a protracted 'good night' to Spice that was concluded only after Zannah had entreated him at least three times to go to his bunk so that she too could go to bed. He went to the cabin he was to share with Mush and undressed by the light of a tiny brass lantern that swung like a pendulum from the deckhead. Mush was already asleep and emitting a short double whistle each time he exhaled which resembled the monotonous call of a chaffinch.

'Here, you'd best give me that thing.' Zannah pushed open the door on his nakedness without batting an eyelid. She indicated a galvanised pail containing two discordantly ticking alarm clocks which stood beside Mush's bunk.

'He reckons he has to have all that lot before it'll wake him,' Zannah told David in response to his look of surprise. 'An' it fairly shakes the boat when it does go off.' She picked up the pail and clocks. 'There's no need for these to disturb you tomorrow. I can wake him myself when the time comes for him to get up.'

She stood in the doorway. David was sitting up in the bunk, his lower half beneath the covers. She surveyed him critically. 'No, no,' she remarked with something like approval. 'You're not nearly such a hairy man as my husband. Not nearly. Spice'll have cause to be thankful for that. Good night.' The door swung to behind her.

He stretched his body in the luxurious proportions of his bunk and felt himself glow with the knowledge that Spice slept only a few strides away from him. Sleep drifted over him with the contemplation of a whole week when nights would be for sleeping and daylight would promise not toil, hazard and exposure, but leisure, tenderness and warmth.

Spice was standing beside him with a cup of tea. Mush's bunk was empty and already made up neatly.

'Christ!' he ejaculated, struggling up. 'Why didn't you wake me earlier?'

'No need,' said Spice. 'A merry Christmas and here's a cup of tea for you.'

'Put it down,' he said, leaning on his elbow and looking at her. 'I've more important things I want to do at the moment.'

'Drink it while it's hot,' she insisted, stepping back.

'Put it down!' he commanded and made to take it from her. With simulated reluctance she put down the cup of tea and went to him.

After breakfast they exchanged presents. Spice was enchanted with her sweater and in return gave him a book on navigation; Zannah presented him with a workmanlike seaman's jersey and Mush shyly handed him a box of cigarettes.

'Now,' said Zannah. 'You two have just time to go to church while I get the dinner.'

David thought at first she was joking, but Spice took a prayer-book from the shelf above the bunk and put it on the table.

'Do you mind?' her eyes asked him and he shook his head reassuringly. She went to her own cabin and came back hatted and coated.

'Surprised?' she asked as they picked their way along the pier.

'Yes,' he admitted. 'I've always thought of Zannah as something of a pagan.'

'Why?' asked Spice. 'Just because she lives in a boat?'

'No, not just that,' he replied. 'She looks too happy to be religious. How often does she insist on your going to church?'

'Only on Christmas Day,' replied Spice. 'She always has insisted and it's become part of Christmas for me now.'

'Does she ever go to church herself?' he asked.

'Who? Aunt Zannah? No.'

'What about Mush?'

'He's away to the church ahead of us.' At David's glance she added: 'Oh yes, he has to go too.'

Perplexed, David shook his head. 'I don't get it,' he confessed. 'Why should she want you and Mush to go to church when she doesn't ever go herself?'

'If you asked her she'd say it's because the only thing religion does for her is to make her hungry and she says her appetite's big enough already.'

David told her of the grim constraint of his parents' religion and of their utter abhorrence of alcohol in any form.

'Not even in case of illness?' she asked with some concern.

'Not ever in illness,' he confirmed.

She looked at him speculatively and as they wiped their feet on the mat in the porch of the church she whispered anxiously: 'They wouldn't take to Zannah or me then, would they?'

As he relaxed in the pew David let his thoughts picture a meeting between his parents and Zannah and Spice. He could envisage his father's tacit disapproval; his mother's tight-lipped horror and her acrid denunciation of them as 'boat women'. He felt Spice looking at him and gave her a small and secret smile.

'What were you thinking of in church, smiling away to yourself?' she teased as they shuffled out with the congregation into the street.

'Of you,' he retorted.

'Of me and who else?' she persisted, squeezing his arm.

For a moment or two he debated whether to tell her.

'What else?' she repeated.

'Of my parents.'

Her face clouded. 'And their not taking to me and Zannah, you mean.'

'Well, yes,' he admitted.

'They wouldn't, would they? Be honest with me, darling.'

'No,' he confessed. 'I don't think they would.'

'Will it make any difference?' Her anxious face was turned up to his and it was all he could do not to halt there and hug her in the presence of the tarrying groups of worshippers.

He laughed. 'Not one scrap,' he assured her, and knew indubitably that it was true.

The smell of Christmas dinner cooking was wafted to them as they came in sight of the pier and hand in hand they began to run towards the *Spizannah*.

'You know, I think Zannah's quite right about religion making one hungry,' he said to Spice as they jumped aboard.

The dinner—the first Christmas dinner he had ever eaten aboard a boat—was superb and Zannah loaded his plate until he pleaded for mercy. Afterwards they listened with rapt attention to the Queen's speech at the conclusion of which Zannah addressed a fervent 'God bless you, sweetheart!' in the direction of the radio. Mush washed the dishes while David and Spice played a frivolous game of dominoes and Zannah delved into cupboards to provide them with dates and figs and nuts and urged upon them her own preserved sugar-plums. The stones from the plums were put into an ash tray and counting them over Spice recited a quaint little rhyme which David had never heard before.

> 'Ickle, Ockle, Blue Bockle,
> Fishes in the sea.
> If you're looking for a lover,
> Please choose me.'

They ate plums until they had the right number of stones to complete the rhyme and ever afterwards they made those last three words their own, invariably adding them in brackets at the end of their letters to each other.

It being a Scottish port Boxing Day was very much business as usual, so taking Spice with him David went in search of a motor-cycle. When he had first propounded the idea of getting a bike Spice had been dubious but when she realised it might mean they could see each other more often she eventually yielded and even managed to work up a semblance of interest in those they inspected. At last David found one that pleased him and which he could afford. They hurried to get it taxed and insured and were soon speeding back to *Spizannah* with Spice a timid pillion passenger.

Zannah and Mush exclaimed delightedly over the bike as David pointed out its robustness.

'I've never been on a motor-bike in my life,' Zannah declared, and seemed to think they should express surprise.

'Well, now's your chance,' David chaffed.

She assessed the machine for a few moments before she said: 'Wait you now till I get a jacket on. Spice! Go and get my jacket for me and a wee bit somethin' to tie over my hair.'

Spice and David looked at each other in consternation.

'Aunt Zannah, you can't!' Spice wailed. 'Look at the size of it compared to you.'

Zannah turned to David. 'I thought you said it was a good strong bike,' she accused.

'It is,' he averred.

'Well, what harm will I do it?'

'None,' he replied, discomfited. 'But . . .'

She cut him short. 'Go and get my jacket, Spice, as I told you.'

But Spice was adamant. 'No, Aunt Zannah. If you try riding pillion you'll both be wobbled into the harbour before you've gone a few yards. You can just stay where you are.'

'Is that right?' asked Zannah.

'It would be a bit tricky,' David temporised. 'You'd best give me more time to get used to it.'

Zannah sighed. 'Oh well, I'll just be content with sitting on it,' she allowed. 'But right enough, when I come to settle on the land maybe something like this will be good for me to get about on.'

Spice relaxed and smiled. Mush's terrified expression gave way to relief.

'Come on,' ordered Zannah, 'let's go below and get some food.'

New Year came quickly. Zannah having spent most of her life in and out of Scottish ports believed in celebrating New Year as assiduously as the Scots do and they began with a bottle of whisky at dinner time. After dinner both Zannah and Mush took to their bunks to sleep off the effects preparatory to commencing the more intensive celebrations in the evening. Spice and David were left to themselves in the fo'c'sle with only the wardship of Zannah's snores to remind them they were not completely alone.

With the last of the daylight came Zannah's friends and acquaintances, all uproariously happy and all brandishing bottles of drink of one kind or another, and soon the fo'c'sle was jammed tight with people who interspersed the leisurely consumption of drams with the eating of 'black bun' and with outbursts of shouting, singing and gesticulation. They were irrepressible; their faces glowed, their eyes grew brighter and moister as the evening progressed and some of the younger ones, complaining of the crush below, went up on deck to dance a couple of reels to the accompaniment of Mush's mouth-organ. When day came there were still revellers aboard, some still clutching half empty bottles as they rested their heads on the table. Others were slouched on the bunks in a stupor. At ten o'clock Zannah started to cook sausages for those who were capable of eating them but it was not until midday that Spice and David ushered the last couple of visitors on to the pier.

'It must have been a good party,' Spice said sleepily as she drew his attention to the number of empty bottles floating about the harbour.

Too soon it was goodbye again. David kicked the bike into life and Spice stood waving from the pier as he drove away. The pillion seemed strangely light without her.

Chapter 16

'Did you have a good New Year?' The greeting went from mouth to mouth throughout the port and on the *Silver Huntress* the next morning the crew were agog to relate their experiences.

'Aye, splendid!' 'Real super!' 'By God! the best yet.' The replies were in every case ecstatic. As they wolfed their pre-breakfast rolls and tea the fo'c'sle was noisy with anecdote.

'I don't believe yon Scully saw his bed from Monday till last night.'

'I didn't see Eggo once. Anybody know what happened to him?'

'By God, the skipper fairly had a drink on him all right. He threw three fellows out of the bar—and threatened to throw the rest out after them.'

'You know the pollis took Gil away for runnin' into a kiosk with his car.'

'That'll cost him somethin'.'

'I hear they found Alex here clinging to a lamp-post on Saturday mornin'. Isn't that right, Alex?'

Alex did not look up from stirring his tea.

'I hear that when the pollis asked him what he was doin' there he told them he was tryin' to keep it warm.'

'Oh, Alex, you're the boy!'

'I don't believe I was there at all,' Alex repudiated at last. He turned to the skipper. 'Was I not with you some time on Saturday mornin'?' he demanded.

'Aye, right enough you were,' confirmed the skipper. 'We went up to Fergy's brother's house.'

'Aye, I thought so,' said Alex.

'Aye, poor man,' intoned the skipper.

'An' was he no' sittin' there by himself in front of the fireplace and not enough fire in to sizzle a man's spit?' asked Alex, intent on consolidating his alibi.

'He was so.'

'That's a terrible thing—not to keep a good fire goin'.' Alex shook his head sadly.

'Well, it was four o'clock in the mornin',' the skipper put in.

'Aye, but it was New Year,' insisted Alex amid a murmur of approval.

'Ach, I daresay his wife wouldn't let him have a fire. She's as queer as a hatter, yon.'

'Fancy sittin' all by himself at New Year, though,' said Chuck in bewilderment.

'He said he had a headache,' said the skipper.

'Ach, the only use his head is to him is for achin',' said Alex.

There was no sign of herring all that day nor the following night and the *Silver Huntress* had ranged well out to sea. The crew began to show signs of a restlessness that was not helped by the radio warnings of imminent force ten gales. They found a small shoal at last and ringed it before the worst of the storm hit them and made further fishing impossible, and sent their neighbour on the long jag back to port with the catch.

'She'll fairly take a tearing,' said the skipper, watching anxiously as the *Silver Venture* ploughed into the seas, covering herself with successive sheets of spray. 'I doubt she'll be back tonight,' he continued, 'so I'd best make for the nearest port. We could lie there till we hear from her and maybe get a few hours' sleep while we have the chance of it.'

Thankfully those who were off watch climbed into their bunks until with the slowing of the engine they were bellowed into activity on deck as the boat was edged into a temporary berth.

'This is a hell of a place,' grumbled Brad. 'The skipper only wants to come here because he hasn't finished his New Year yet.'

David thought it looked indeed 'a hell of a place', with nothing but a jumble of buildings looming through the rain and mist like derelicts.

'Comin' ashore?' asked the skipper, who, though he could not have had more than two hours sleep in the past thirty-six hours seemed eager to revisit a place he claimed he had not set foot in for a couple of years.

'The women here is pretty easy,' he added, as an incentive to Brad.

Josh, the boy, and David were keen enough to go. Brad came moodily. The skipper stopped at the nearest pub where he was immediately recognised by several of the customers who came forward to shake his hand and wish him 'Happy New Year'. The drinks came swiftly.

'I'm scunnered of drink,' said Brad, after swallowing two or three. 'If I take any more I'll fetch up all my dinner.'

David looked at him in surprise.

'New Year always does this to me,' he admitted. 'I drink so much that I hate the smell of the stuff for a while afterwards.'

'Let's take a look round, then,' David suggested. 'The skipper'll not be in a hurry to move for a while yet.'

They trudged out into the stormy street, looking into shop windows and wondering what to do with themselves to pass the time.

'Where did Josh get to, did you notice?' Brad asked.

'Don't know,' David replied. 'I saw him take a drink but then I think he went off somewhere.'

'Maybe he's away back to the boat,' said Brad. They went into a dismal-looking tea-room and drank a dismal cup of tea. Brad chatted up the waitress half-heartedly and showed no inclination to linger, so they bought fresh milk and rolls and cakes to take back to the boat. As the shops began to light up for the evening they went to collect the skipper. He was still at the bar where they had left him, a glass of whisky in front of him and a covey of friends gathered about.

'Come on, you bloody slobs!' he greeted Brad and David hilariously. 'Take a drink and make men of yourselves. What've you been up to anyway, tartin' around.' They had to take another dram with him before they could get him to leave the bar. Once outside he appeared to sober up immediately so that David suspected his drunkenness was often only an attitude.

On their way back to the pier they came upon a cluster of Salvationists at the corner of the street, their preacher trying valiantly to make himself heard above the noise of the wind. One of the men approached with a collecting box and with a muttered oath the skipper delved beneath his oilskin and magnanimously produced a handful of silver. Selecting two half-crowns he dropped them into the box.

'They wouldn't do very well here if it wasn't for folks like me,' he explained with a grin.

'Here, look at that!' Brad exclaimed, and startled by his tone David and Big Cam turned to look in the direction he indicated.

'Look at what?' demanded Big Cam.

'That's Josh, that is,' said Brad, pointing to a figure which stood sheltering in a doorway a short distance from the band. 'We'd best go and get him, hadn't we?'

The skipper stared suspiciously at Josh who appeared to be engrossed by what the preacher was saying.

'Nah,' said the skipper after a moment's thought. 'Leave him be. So long as he doesn't go any closer to them than that they'll not do him any harm.'

There was no message from the *Silver Venture* when they returned and the weather forecast warned of increasing winds.

'I think we'd best make up our minds we'll be here for the weekend,' said the skipper.

'Of all the bloody luck!' exploded Brad.

Chuck said, 'I don't fancy it myself,' and looked at the sea. Alex agreed. 'It's too coarse altogether. We're better off where we are.'

They went ashore again and bought more stores in case of emergency and the next morning the skipper said: 'Maybe when the tide drops there'll be a lull long enough to get out of here and go somewhere else.'

'Where else?' asked Brad sceptically.

'There's a wee harbour I know of at the back of one of the islands.'

'Where one of your relatives lives, I suppose,' muttered Brad.

'Aye, as a matter of fact, old Farquhar is by way of being a bit of a relative,' acknowledged the skipper. 'An' I'd like to take him his New Year.'

Brad humphed. 'Well, it's either that or havin' all your friends here droppin' in on us and spoiling us for our sleep,' he said.

At low tide the *Silver Huntress* nosed her way out of the harbour, leaping to meet the translucent walls of white-fanged water that reared themselves at her bows. Like a crazy lift she plummeted into the deep troughs that rolled away from her stern. The engine was throttled down but even so the water cascaded over her decks so that the boat seemed to be as much under the sea as above it. Visibility was nil. Everything was battened down, the rest of the crew being in the fo'c'sle. In the wheelhouse the ship to ship radio crackled and boomed sporadically and, wedged in a corner, David watched each wave as it came, half expecting that before long one would catch the boat unawares and swamp her. But the skipper, his face grim with concentration, pulled her to meet the seas, crying out at her stubbornness if she did not yield instantly to the helm, exulting when she rose buoyantly to ride a more menacing one than the rest. The boat rode on, staggering sometimes at the impact of a sea but always defeating it until the abrasive fear that had made David feel sore all over was replaced by the confident acceptance of the boat's ability to take it in her stride.

After an hour or so the seas shortened perceptibly and they were able to catch fleeting glimpses of land through the thick squalls of rain. The skipper relaxed.

'Now this fellow I mentioned, Farquhar,' he began, his sentences coming in short breathless jerks as he pulled at the wheel. 'Like I said, he's a kind of relative of mine. Fine fellow too, though he must be nearer eighty than seventy. Did a couple of years in gaol some time back.'

'What for?' David asked.

'Supposed to have stolen some furniture from a big house on one of the islands.'

'And had he?'

'He confessed to it. He couldn't have done it, but he confessed to it, so they put him in gaol.'

David waited patiently for the explanation.

'This big house was on an island all by itself,' went on the skipper, 'and was only lived in for about three weeks of the year. Well, the folk found when they came to it one year that most of the furniture was missing. Big heavy stuff it was too, old fashioned, you know, that they'd bought along with the house many years before. Well, they told the pollis and the pollis visited all the nearby islands searching for the stuff and askin' plenty questions, but they didn't find anythin'. It wasn't till a year or two later some of the folks from another island brought over a party to ceilidh with Farquhar and his friends and of course it being a nice summer night a couple of the young lads and lassies went off to find a quiet place to do some courtin'. They must have found somethin' but they didn't let on till they got back to their own homes and then one of the lads started sayin' he'd found a cave with a wonderful bird's nest in it over on the island. Birds the like of which he'd never seen before, he said. Of course, everybody guessed what he meant right enough but they wouldn't have let it go any further except that one of the children must have overheard and got excited about these wonderful birds. He told his friends at school about them. Somehow or other the pollis heard of it and twigged and started askin' questions again. Nobody would admit to anythin' so they went off to Farquhar's island to search and there in one of the caves they found the furniture all neatly stored. Everybody else denied knowing anything about it but Farquhar, he just said yes, he'd taken it. "You an' who else?" they asked him but Farquhar insisted he'd done it all by himself. Of course, they didn't believe him for he was past sixty by then and he only had a dinghy. They knew it just wasn't possible for one man to carry great big things like wardrobes and sideboards, load them into a dinghy and row two or three miles across the sea with them. Anyway, they knew Farquhar and knew he'd never been known to do a dishonest thing in his life. But Farquhar insisted he'd done it himself and they couldn't do anything else but charge him. He got two years for it.'

'What made him take the blame?' David demanded.

'I don't know anything but what my father told me,' admitted the skipper. 'But he says when he next saw Farquhar again he asked him point blank why he'd taken the blame when everybody knew it was his two sons who'd done the whole job and not said a word to the old man till it was found.'

'And what did Farquhar say?'

'My father said Farquhar just looked at him and said, "My sons are young and to go to prison might have sent them bad for the rest of their lives. I'm an old man, too old to go bad now, so what difference would a prison sentence make to me"?'

'But you'd have thought the two sons would have owned up and not let him suffer for them,' David said indignantly.

'Aye, you might have thought that,' agreed the skipper. 'But it was Farquhar who went to prison so it seems they didn't.'

'What happened to his sons?'

'Oh, they went away. One of them was killed in the war and the other died not long after in an accident. Farquhar never saw them again. Maybe they'd have lived longer if they'd served their sentence. They were always a bit on the wild side, though.'

The *Silver Huntress* turned towards the land and a narrow cliff-sheltered harbour opened up before them. As soon as they had dropped anchor a boat was being rowed out from the shore. It came alongside and an old man stood up, holding on to the *Silver Huntress*'s gunwale.

The skipper greeted him and introduced David. Farquhar looked the typical old crofter, tranquil-eyed, white-haired, with a skin like weathered rope. His shoulders were slightly bent and there was about him an air of quiet dignity. David tied the dinghy at the stern and Farquhar clambered up on deck. They all went below to take another New Year dram along with mugs of tea and a long exchange of gossip. After about an hour Farquhar stood up.

'Well now, you'll all be comin' ashore to take your New Year with me and the cailleach,' he invited.

Chick maintained he was too sleepy to go anywhere and Fergy elected to stay and keep an eye on the boat. The rest of the crew piled into Farquhar's dinghy and pulling with strong, expert strokes the old man rowed them ashore. They followed him along a rough track that wound over the hill and down again into an exposed bay where several stone houses, roofed with tired thatch or black corrugated iron, were dotted around the shore.

In the doorway of the cottage they were approaching a small boy stood watching them. A black and white collie gyrated in front of him, barking at the appearance of strangers. Farquhar reprimanded the dog and spoke gently to the boy in Gaelic. The boy nodded and bounded away to watch from the safety of a shed.

'Come away in,' Farquhar said, and led the way into a small dark room where a fire of peat and driftwood sent flames licking at the bottom of a hanging kettle. On the table were set out plates of girdle scones, oatcakes, cheese, and biscuits and jam.

'Have you no' got the tea made?' Farquhar addressed the pale-faced, twitching-mouthed old woman who sat in a hard wooden chair beside the fire. She muttered fretfully in Gaelic and taking up the poker rattled it among the peats. There were no spoken introductions as the men went forward to shake her hand and wish her a 'Happy New Year' but she smiled at them and nodded and when Big Cam spoke to her in Gaelic her eyes lit with pleasure.

David sat with Brad and Josh on a long wooden bench beneath the tiny window. The child Hamish stood beside the old woman's chair and watched them surreptitiously, bobbing down out of sight behind the chair whenever David caught his eye and offered a smile. He could only have been about four years old but his grandfather spoke to him as if he were three times that age.

'Away and get a bitty more wood for the fire, Hamish,' he

commanded. 'And see it's dry now. The last lot was awful wet.' The boy darted outside and returned clutching a pile of driftwood which he dropped into the hearth. 'Now some peats,' the old man instructed and off he went again, this time bringing back a pail of peats. When he was not occupied on errands Hamish struggled with some pieces cut from old rubber boots which he was endeavouring to tie up in the shape of a ball. David tried to coax him to let him help, and eventually Hamish came, proffering the bundle and remaining to stand beside David to watch him bind the rubber with odd lengths of string. David tried to bounce the makeshift ball on the floor and though it showed little resilience Hamish snatched it up delightedly and ran with it outside.

There came the noise of boots thudding and a shuffling in the doorway. Two men entered, one of them Farquhar's nephew, a young man of about twenty, the other a handsome well-built fellow who put great vigour into his handshake but who otherwise acknowledged their salutations by many smiles and much nodding of his head. It transpired that he was dumb and though his expression was alert enough when attention was focussed on him at other times his face became vacant, his mouth gaping open.

More people came shuffling and stamping into the room until the whole population—about a dozen souls in all—were gathered to drink tea and whisky, to hear news of other places and to recount their own doings. Memories groped further into the past. 'I mind my father telling me . . .' and then, 'My grandfather minded that happening himself.' Inevitably someone hummed a snatch of song and soon they were all singing the nostalgic Gaelic songs of their youth while their feet beat time gently on the floor. David was thoroughly enjoying the experience but Brad grew restless.

'How about comin' and havin' a look at the rest of the island?' he suggested. 'The weather's not too bad for it now.'

They went out and though no one commented on or even seemed to notice their departure before they had gone very far David looked back and was in time to see Hamish, the dog at his heels, dodge quickly behind a remnant of dry-stone wall not very far behind. He turned again after a little while and saw the same thing happening. It was obvious the child was trying to follow them. Brad noticed it too.

'What's the little bastard want?' he muttered, and shouted at Hamish: 'Are you wantin' with us?'

Self-consciously Hamish came out from his hiding-place and stood looking at them.

'Come on, if you're comin'. But we're not stoppin' to wait for you, mind,' Brad told him.

With shy eagerness the child ran to join them and only part heedful of his fat little legs struggling along beside them Brad and David trudged on, skirting peat bogs and pulling their way through thickets of brambles. The wind gusted through the corries and snuffled among the brittle heather and though the rain had ceased the prostrated sedge was still weighted with shiny droplets that polished their sea-boots to a mirror-like shine. They started to climb to the highest point of the island and as they reached the crest of the hill the wind hit them with a suddenness that made them glad to turn and lean back against its strength as a policeman leans against a thrusting crowd. As Hamish came up it caught him and rolled him over several times in a comical flurry of arms and legs. He made no sound as David pulled him to his feet but he was biting his lips to keep back the tears. With a stab of compunction David realised that the poor little mite had tired himself out trying to keep up with them. Dusk was approaching and it was time they started back again.

'Have you ever had a "piggy-back"?' David asked. Hamish did not answer but only looked at him mutely.

'I don't suppose he knows much English,' suggested Brad. David bent down. 'Now, you climb on my back and pretend I'm a pig that you're riding to market.' Brad hoisted the child on to David's back. 'Hold on to the collar of my jacket and don't struggle.' Obediently he did as he was told.

'How's that now?' Brad asked him with brusque interest.

'Fine,' Hamish whispered. That was the only word David ever heard him speak. They plodded on downhill and then up again to take them over the last rise that would bring them in sight of the cottages. They were about half way up when David felt the warm wet trickle seeping through his clothes, running down his legs and into his boots. It took him a moment to grasp what had happened. He almost flung Hamish from his back in his haste to get rid of him.

'You filthy little bastard!' he roared at him in disgust. 'Why didn't you say you wanted to pee instead of doing it all down my back?'

The dog growled at David's tone. Brad flung himself on a patch of heather, convulsed with laughter. Hamish looked abjectly from David to Brad and ran to the dog for comfort.

'That's the last blasted time I'll ever take pity on you, you thankless little horror!' David threatened, although already the sight of the child's face was begging to make him relent. Poor little devil must have been wanting to do it even before he'd picked him up, he thought, but he'd been too shy to say so and too afraid of being left behind on the moors in the dark if he'd stopped long enough on his own. With a sob Hamish fled, scrambling up the hill and leaving David shaking his jacket and tipping up his boots.

Brad recovered himself. 'There must be somethin' about you that makes for peein',' he chaffed. 'First Bessie's dog and now Hamish. By God, but you'll be well pickled!'

David did not go back to the cottage but went straight to the harbour and rowed himself out to the boat to sluice himself down and wash out his clothes. When the rest returned he was in his bunk, his washing tied to the lowered mast.

By morning the gale had moderated but the forecast warned that it was only temporary. The wind was expected to increase again and veer.

'That means it'll blow right in here,' said the skipper, 'so we may as well make for home. The *Silver Huntress* will ride a stern sea till Kingdom Come.'

David went to rescue his still damp clothes from the mast.

'That was a bit of luck—good or bad, whichever you like to think of it,' teased the skipper. 'Brad tells me you're after makin' a bit of a habit of that kind of thing.'

David told him what he thought of people who allowed their children to grow up incontinent.

'Aye, but he's not used to strangers,' the skipper interceded. 'Likely he wouldn't know the English for telling you what he wanted.'

'I could have understood that need in any language,' David retorted.

'Ach, you can't blame the kid,' said the skipper. 'Nobody bothers much about him except Farquhar and he wouldn't be thinkin' of anythin' like that happenin' now, would he?'

'Whose child is he, anyway?' David asked.

'It's their daughter's. She went away to Glasgow to work. She was supposed to have got married there but nobody's ever seen her husband. She just turned up with the baby and dumped him with his grandparents and that was that. She's never shown an interest in him since—though likely she'll want him back when he's old enough to start earnin'!'

'Old Farquhar seems to specialise in making up for his family's mistakes,' David remarked.

'Aye, he's a bit of a saint, you might say,' agreed the skipper. 'But all the same, it's hard on the child. The old cailleach's poorly a lot of the time and with there bein' no other children on the island Hamish has no company, except for his dog.'

David began to feel ashamed of his vehement chiding of the child and remembering his poor toy of tied rubber resolved that next time he was in port he would buy a ball and keep it on board ready for when he should see Hamish again.

Chapter 17

True to the forecast the wind went round to the south and increased in fury. *Silver Huntress* tossed restlessly in the harbour along with the rest of the fleet, while her crew kicked around, exasperated by the inaction and gloomily predicting the thinness of their next week's pay packets. After three and a half days, however, the wind had dropped and the forecast promised light breezes and good visibility. With the impetuousness of released greyhounds the boats raced out of the harbour. The herring season was coming to an end and consequently shoals were smaller and more difficult to locate so that it was with surprised pleasure that the crew of the *Silver Huntress* heard the familiar call to stand by.

'Trust Big Cam,' said Brad happily. 'He'll find herrin' where another skipper would swear there wasn't a chance of it.'

The herring was there but their neighbour boat, *Silver Venture*, was not yet close enough and they cruised around 'mindin' the shoal', as Brad put it, until the golden rim of the sunset had been smothered by violet clouds and the gulls had given up prospecting and gone to their resting-places. The crew stood on deck, flapping their arms and trying to keep warm.

When the *Silver Venture* appeared they found the herring to be in several small shoals and they ringed until dawn before their catch was big enough to satisfy the skipper. David and Brad watched the *Silver Venture* starting on her return trip to the port and the market.

'Aye, well, there'll be a wage in it for us—just,' Brad murmured.

They were near enough to Farquhar's island to make for the shelter of the bay where they could lie for a couple of hours while they had a meal and a brief rest before it was time to begin the search for herring again. The skipper steered towards it, the anchor splashed over and the boat swung to meet the breeze. The sea was no more than rumpled where she lay but around the shore of the island the ill-humoured remnants of the recent storm still plunged and broke in a frieze of white foam. Before leaving the deck Big Cam turned to survey the drab houses against their backcloth of hills hung with shreds of mist like discarded combings from the grey sky.

'Hello!' he said suddenly, and Fergy, who was just about to go below, stopped to discover the cause of the skipper's exclamation. David also paused and saw two figures who were dragging a dinghy over the piled tangle that the storm had wrested from its deep sea roots. Twice the men tried to launch the boat and twice the breaking swell lifted it, driving it broadside on back to the shore, before they could jump in and grab the oars. At the third attempt, however, the men succeeded in getting aboard and with strong, quick pulls managed to row clear of the breakers and head in the direction of the *Silver Huntress*.

'What the hell do these bastards want?' muttered Fergy truculently. 'They've had their New Year, surely?'

'Well, they're not likely to go to all this trouble just for a fry,' said Big Cam in a puzzled voice.

'That's what I'm thinkin',' agreed Fergy.

They were accustomed to visitors coming out from the shore to accept a fry of herring in return for a gift of fresh milk or potatoes but it was usually only in calm weather they came and then not until they had given the crew time for an hour or two's rest.

As the boat came alongside David recognised old Farquhar and his nephew, Torquil, at the oars and despite the glow of exertion on their faces they looked unnaturally grave. The skipper and Fergy crouched down by the gunwale to listen to their excuse for coming out but David, deciding that it was probably only some message to be sent over the radio or some instructions for one of the shops in the port, gave them only a brief nod of acknowledgment before going below. A minute or two later the crew in the fo'c'sle looked at each other in surprise as they heard the engine start and a shout from Fergy to get the anchor aboard.

'Oh God! What next?' said Brad irascibly.

Murmuring, he and David went on deck, their irritation giving way to bewilderment as they saw Farquhar and Torquil standing beside the wheelhouse and their dinghy tied astern.

'What's all this, then?' demanded Brad of Fergy.

'We're goin' to collect a coffin,' Fergy snapped.

'A coffin? Why us?'

'Because there's nobody else to do it. The telephone's not workin' and their own launch got damaged in the storm.' Fergy went back to the wheelhouse.

'I suppose it's the old cailleach,' said David. 'She looked pretty frail.'

Brad muttered a testy condemnation of old cailleachs who had the temerity to die so inconveniently. He kicked at a coil of rope. 'It's no' right that we should have to go,' he fumed. 'Fishin's one thing. Playin' at hearses is another.'

They went below to finish their meal and to impart the purpose of their mission to Chick and the rest.

'I hope they're not thinkin' of puttin' the coffin aboard this boat,' he expostulated. 'If they do we may just as well pack it in, for there'll be no herrin' comin' to our nets till the end of the season.' He hurried up on deck as if to make his objection and Brad and David stayed drinking tea until they heard the engine slowing down and the dinghy being cast off. When they decided it was time to go and find out what was happening the dinghy was already returning. At first they thought Farquhar was coming to tell them they had not managed to get the coffin after all but Brad gave a startled exclamation as he noticed something tucked beneath the bow thwart. Simultaneously David, Brad and Chick turned to one another with stunned disbelief. The coffin was no more than three feet long: a child's coffin. No, no, not Hamish; the protest rose to David's throat but he did not speak. But it was for Hamish: Chick, who had dashed to the wheelhouse for enlightenment, confirmed it in a voice that was ragged with phlegm. He spat into the sea.

'But he peed down your back only last Thursday!' The rebuttal burst from Brad as if the incident should have given the child some sort of immunity. There was a glint of tragic humour in the glance David and Chick exchanged. In silence they watched the dinghy come alongside, leaving it to Fergy to hold the rope and see the two men aboard. The coffin was left where it was.

The skipper made for the island. Alex and Josh had come up and commiserating they clustered around while Farquhar told them between long pauses what had happened.

The men of the village had gone off to round up the sheep and had left the boy with his grandmother. Soon after they had gone Hamish had announced in the mature way he so often assumed that he was going to try to catch a fish for her dinner, and taking his usual hazel stick and string and hooks he had gone off to his favourite fishing-place—a slab of rock which jutted out from the shore. He had gone there so often in the past that his grandmother had not worried in the least when he did not return for his 'piece' at midday. She had not been feeling well, Farquhar explained, and she probably had not noticed the time passing. However, when Farquhar and Torquil had returned later in the afternoon and there was still no sign of Hamish they suspected that something was wrong and had immediately gone in search of him. They had not needed to look far. Even before they reached the rock the dog had called their attention to something floating on the water. They thought Hamish must have slipped and hit his head and thus stunned had rolled over the edge of the rock into the sea. It was shallow there, but it had been deep enough.

'You see, we'd taken the dog with us to the sheep,' Farquhar told them distractedly. He was convinced that if the dog had been with Hamish it would have somehow contrived to save him.

It had all happened on the Saturday following the Thursday when the *Silver Venture*'s crew had visited the house. Now it was Wednesday and in the small 'but and ben' of a cottage with its one living room and one bedroom the keeping of the body was becoming a problem.

The skipper went forward and called David to join him.

'Beardie, you might just as well come along ashore with me and give a hand,' he proposed.

'What with?' asked David, perplexed.

'Gettin' him boxed up an' that.'

'Okay,' David agreed reluctantly.

'I've said I'll take them to the burial ground. There's not one here so it's the least I can do seein' as I'm a sort of relative of his. I reckon if we're smart we can get back here before the *Silver Venture* is ready for us.' He looked over his shoulder as if to see whether they were being watched and then went on confidentially: 'As a matter of fact, that's why it's best I go with them, just to make sure they don't waste any time. These two would be all right . . .' he nodded in the direction of the old man and his nephew, 'but the women's likely to be a nuisance. They get that worked up.'

David had a fleeting vision of himself fencing off a covey of wailing women and wondered just what he might be expected to do.

'Will they be able to get a minister?' he asked as the thought struck him.

'They had a missionary out the night he was drowned. He came over with the doctor. He's not likely to be comin' again, I doubt.'

In a steady drizzle of rain they were rowed ashore and while Torquil and Farquhar went off in the direction of the houses to acquaint the neighbours with the news that the funeral was about to take place David and Big Cam carried the coffin between them into a drystone shed that appeared to be partly dairy, partly peat store.

'He kind of took a fancy to you,' said the skipper as he moved a setting bowl of milk from an old table and David placed the coffin on its poppy-patterned linoleum top. There came the sound of slow, heavy footsteps and David stood back as Farquhar, carrying a stiff sheet-wrapped bundle and followed by the collie dog, came into the shed. The old man's nod indicated that he needed no help with the task he had to do. Big Cam leaned against the door-jamb and stared out at the sea with angry, accusing eyes. Torquil came and propped himself against the piled peats. The dog lay watchful and anxious. Farquhar worked resolutely and when he took up the lid of the coffin he paused for only a moment to look into the child's still face. David turned away as the lid was pressed firmly down. He knew that the gloomy shed with its rough shingle floor, the small coffin resting on its garish linoleum base, and the sound of the whimpering dog backed by the crashing swell and the intermittent wailing of gulls, had stamped itself indelibly on his mind.

'That's it, then.' The old man's voice was completely matter-of-fact. Big Cam turned abruptly.

'Right, we'll take this now,' he told Farquhar, disguising

his own emotion by the assumption of impatience. 'You go to the house and tell the women we're ready for off. We've not that much time to spare.' He and David took up the coffin, handling it as gently as they could while their boots slipped and slithered over the tangle-strewn shingle and the dog impeded their progress by running in front of them, barking incessantly. The skipper swore at it and it slunk behind. When they reached the water's edge they put the coffin down on the shingle while they waited for Farquhar and Torquil. In front of the cottage David could see a group of women standing in attitudes of conventional grief. He wondered if Hamish's mother was among them and muttered the question to Big Cam.

'Not very like,' said Big Cam. 'How would she have got?'

Farquhar and Torquil, who had now exchanged their gumboots and oilskins for ordinary leather boots and gabardine raincoats and who were both wearing new-looking tweed caps, picked up the coffin and gently wedged it again under a thwart in the dinghy. With almost as much gentleness Torquil laid two spades along the floorboards and seizing their chance in a lull of the swell they launched the boat and all four leaped in. The dog began to howl.

Fergy had already started the engine of the *Silver Huntress* and as soon as they had climbed aboard and the dinghy, still holding its small burden, had been tied astern, they began to steam slowly away. Not until the houses had disappeared from sight behind a point of land did the skipper give the order to increase speed.

At the unkempt burial ground almost at the sea's edge Farquhar prospected for a suitable spot and they took it in turns to dig the small grave. Torquil lowered the coffin into it and the old man produced a prayer-book from his pocket and held it towards Big Cam.

'You'll read a piece from this?' he asked him.

The unexpectedness of the request discomfited the skipper momentarily but taking the book he began to read where Farquhar had indicated, his words coming hastily at first and then slowing as he became more composed.

David studied him covertly, wondering at the incongruity of the spectacle of this burly man, so frequently and so rumbustiously drunk; so habitually and so unregenerately blasphemous; now standing in this rain-misted, grey-walled cemetery with its confusion of untended mounds and listing stones, and deputising for a man of God beside the open grave. With the rain glistening on his yellow oilskin he stood in much the same attitude as he adopted when bawling profanity on his own deck.

'May he find acceptance in Thy sight . . .' His reading again gathered momentum and the last few words of the prayer were a hurried gabble.

'Right then,' he said, resuming his air of impatience. 'Give me a spade.' He handed the prayer-book back to Farquhar.

Back in the bay Farquhar thanked David for his help and his attendance at the funeral. David's tongue groped for suitable words of condolence.

'It was a terrible bad blow we had,' the old man said as he climbed back into his dinghy.

'It was that,' David agreed with miserable inadequacy.

'Aye, force nine the wireless said, and I believe we got the full strength of it hereabouts too.' He made a gesture of farewell as the dinghy was cast off and *Silver Huntress* surged impatiently forward.

In the fo'c'sle Fergy was by himself flicking through a magazine. He looked up as David entered.

'So you got back,' he commented.

'Aye,' David grunted, surprised at the acknowledgment of his presence. He was aware of Fergy watching him as he fumbled in his bunk for a packet of cigarettes.

'Here, have one of these,' Fergy said, with unprecedented

affability and extracting a cigarette from his own packet he threw it across to David.

'Thanks,' said David, as Fergy struck a match and held it for him. He wondered at the change in Fergy's manner and put it down to the fact that he was probably looking as tired and strained as he felt.

'Any tea in that pot?' he asked.

'Aye, plenty,' Fergy said, preparing to go up on deck. With one foot on the ladder he turned and without looking at David said: 'I'll tell you somethin', Beardie. What's happened today will make me glad to see my little bugger at the week-end.'

'I'll bet,' David responded. He tried to catch Fergy's eye but Fergy was already halfway up the steps.

The next weekend Fergy invited him to go and take tea with himself and his family.

Chapter 18

Two years went by and he was still in the port; still determined to remain a fisherman. During the lobster seasons he had worked with Noddy in the *Fair Lassie* and when the winter herring had come in he had been fortunate enough to get a berth on one or other of the herring boats for at least a good part of the season. He had become virtually indistinguishable from all the other tough, yellow-oilskinned, sea-booted fraternity of the port who came in with salt roughened faces and stiff smiles each weekend and departed with terse comments and eyes appraising the weather each Monday morning. His body had become thoroughly adjusted to a life that could be summarised as toiling, eating and sporadically sleeping for the greater part of the week; it had grown indifferent to cold; accustomed to being constantly bounced up and down when he tried to relax in his bunk, and now it accepted without protest the long hours of hauling whether he was cramped over a prodigiously full stomach or over an achingly empty one. His senses had sharpened, his ears being always alert for the noise of breakers; his eyes ever watchful for the gradations of darkness on the water that might mean a submerged rock or might only be a deepening ripple in the tide. Without effort his walk had become the short careful stump of the fisherman who is more often than not negotiating decks that are treacherous with slime, and his limbs had developed a confluence with the motion of the boat so that except in the most turbulent weather he was as much at ease in her as he would have been on land.

He had learned to know the sea so that he could accept its moods of wanton savagery with only a little less complacency than he accepted its moods of sunlit meekness; he could recognise the shapes of waves well enough to help the boat combat their tactics when he took his turn at the helm. He scanned each dawn with the same shrewd interest with which he scanned his watch and reckoned he was well able to deduce the likely weather from the appearance of a sunset as were the rest of the fishermen.

He knew all the crews of all the boats that habitually used the port; he knew what most of them earned and what they drank. In the pub as among the testy companionship of tired men in the fo'c'sle he had learned to avoid contentious subjects. And he had learned to swear; his tongue was now unsurpassed at rattling out an exchange of malediction that two years previously would have made his ears burn.

Perhaps it was the relief of being able to vent his anger and frustration in fluent invective; perhaps it was the constant hazard of his life; perhaps it was the balm of being surrounded by glorious scenery or perhaps it was just being in love, but he realised that he was becoming more tolerant. He began to be uncomfortably aware of his own shortcomings; to think sympathetically of his parents and even to acknowledge a genuine albeit tepid desire to make his peace with them.

Spice was also urging him to bring the estrangement to an end, for they were now engaged to be married and it bothered her that his parents were still in ignorance of it. He still hesitated, however, thinking there was yet plenty of time before he need make a move towards reconciliation, Zannah having insisted on a two-year engagement because she considered Spice at barely nineteen too young to marry. She also made it plain that David's living was too precarious for her to be enthusiastic about the prospect of their marrying earlier. Meantime Spice, at the suggestion of someone who had seen her paintings in the fo'c'sle of the *Spizannah*, had been packed off to art school in Glasgow.

'She might just as well have her chance now,' Zannah had told David. 'When she's married she'll maybe be too taken up with a family to have time for paintin'.'

'That's very likely,' agreed David. He had felt a twinge of jealousy at the idea of Spice going to join a bevy of fancy-free students at an art college, but the twinge soon vanished when he realised that she would no longer be itinerant and they would stand far more chance of contriving meetings than they did when he had to chase off each weekend to the different ports where the *Spizannah* might be discharging.

Autumn had come and because of bad weather in the late summer the lobster season had finished early and so far the herring had not begun to shoal in quantities big enough to tempt out all the boats that would later be in pursuit. The prophecies were for a poor season and as a result David found himself without a berth or even the promise of one for the winter. Because he was unhappy away from the boats David was on the pier watching what signs of activity there were when he noticed a stranger who seemed to be inspecting the moored boats with more than the usual tourist curiosity.

'Who's the bod?' he asked a passing trolleyman.

'Dunno,' replied the man. 'Likely he's wantin' to buy a boat. That's what they're usually after up here at this time of year.' The porter trundled his load away.

Brad appeared, carrying a cluster of brightly coloured net-floats which he threw aboard the *Silver Huntress*. The 'King', of course, was fishing, baffling the other skippers by finding shoals 'God knows where' and as a result keeping his crew contented. David repeated his question to Brad.

'He's from South Africa, so he says,' Brad replied. 'I had a word with him earlier on and he's been tellin' me he's tourin'' around all the ports seein' the different ways of fishin' we have in this country.'

The stranger, seeing Brad and David watching him, sauntered towards them.

'Says his name's Nelson Farr,' Brad muttered under his breath, and added, 'Seems a nice enough chap.'

'Things are pretty quiet here,' Nelson Farr observed, nodding to David. 'Does it get more lively than this, any time?' While Brad hastened to assure him that 'when the herrin' really starts to come you'll see this place fairly jump to life', David noted the good but not impeccable clothes, the taut figure, the weathered eyes set deep in a face tanned to the gold-brown of onion skin by a deep probing sun that had left no winter-white creases. He was aware of Brad saying, 'You can walk from one side of this harbour to the other across the boats when we're real busy.'

Nelson Farr accepted the statement with a shrewd glance at the meagre assembly of boats and asked questions about the size of the fleet normally fishing, average catches and prices and the process of marketing. In return he told them of his own fleet of boats in South Africa and gave them mouth watering descriptions of the wages earned by the crews. His voice had a colonial twang but it was without the brash overtone David had expected to hear.

A hail from the *Silver Huntress* took Brad hurrying back to her and at Farr's suggestion David and he continued their conversation at the bar in the pub. Farr disclosed that he had started fishing ten years previously with an old tub of a boat and had by dint of long hours and every sort of economy built up his fleet to some half-dozen boats, each manned by a native crew under a white skipper. His present tour was not only to investigate the different fishing methods but also to include a visit to a yard where he was having a boat built to his own design. David recognised it as the achievement of a dream.

'How about you?' Nelson Farr asked. 'How long have you been fishing?'

David told him of the circumstances of his own initiation into the life of a fisherman; of his obsession with it and of his ambition some day to become skipper of his own boat.

'You've not got a berth yourself at the moment?' Farr asked.

'No,' admitted David, 'but I'm pretty sure I'll get one once the herring does come in. If it does,' he added morosely.

'And if it doesn't?'

David grimaced and leaned his arm on the bar counter. 'Then it's hard times,' he said. 'I'll just have to kick around and see if something else turns up.'

Farr stared into his half-empty glass for a few moments before tossing down the remains of his drink.

'How long d'you reckon it will take you to get your own boat, supposing you keep in steady work?' he asked.

David sucked in his breath. 'Oh, say six, maybe seven years if I'm lucky and if I'm careful. Maybe more. It depends what sort of boat I'll be content with. It won't be a new one, of course.'

'You haven't thought of trying somewhere else to fish?' Farr called for another drink.

'Fishing's pretty chancy everywhere I believe,' David told him. 'I'm best to stay where I'm known.'

'I didn't mean another port. I meant another country.' David felt Farr was watching him closely.

'Where, for instance?'

'South Africa,' said Farr. 'I could use another skipper.' Their glances met appraisingly. 'Two years skipper for me and I reckon you'd be well on the way to owning your own boat,' Farr continued. 'Is there any chance of your doing that by staying here?'

'Christ, no!' David ejaculated and felt his head spin. 'Honest?'

'I'd reckon so.'

'It's hard to believe that,' David said as if he were talking to himself.

'It's possible,' reiterated his companion. 'No, more than just possible,' he corrected. 'You don't have to search for your fish there as you have to here and the demand's always bigger than the supply. I don't think you'd be much short of getting a boat if you're prepared to work for it.'

'Two years,' David repeated bemusedly. Though not questioning his instinctive trust of the man he was puzzled why so brief an acquaintance should result in his being offered such an opportunity.

'Why me?' he demanded of Farr. 'I might be a "green-hand" for all you know. Or just a hanger-on bastard that only gets the chance of a berth when there's no other able-bodied man available.'

Farr's tight line of mouth twitched with amusement. 'I've met a couple of skippers already and talked to them,' he replied. 'I told them I was looking for a likely chap and they seemed to think you might be interested.'

'So,' said David, 'you found out about me before you made the offer?'

'I can't afford altruism,' responded Farr. 'I'm making you an offer of a two-year contract, passage paid if you want to consider it.'

Two years! Forsake Spice for two long years! Could he? But there'd be enough to buy his own boat by the time he did see her again and they could be married straight away. His thoughts leaped over the hurdles of impossibility. He let himself think of having his own boat; of having a permanent and indisputable stake in the plundering of the sea. Desire consumed him, overcoming his initial diffidence and rejecting the thrusts of dismay at the thought of the long separation from Spice.

'Think about it,' Nelson Farr said, looking at his watch.

'But I'd want to have your answer by Friday. It's not giving you much time but I'm away to the east coast now for a day or two. After that it's the south of England to look at my new boat and then the plane back home. If you're coming back with me I'll need to book your passage.'

'I'll certainly think about it,' David promised whole-heartedly, knowing that the offer was going to torment him until it was settled one way or another.

He decided to go and see Spice the following day and find out her reaction to the project. He set out on his motor-cycle in a yellow dawn with the sun rising as imposingly as if it had just been launched with champagne. Spice's expression when she saw him so unexpectedly waiting for her outside the college was so ecstatic that he doubted for a time whether he could bring himself to think more of the offer, let alone voice it.

'There's nothing wrong, is there?' she asked when he had hugged her.

'Nothing at all,' he assured her.

She looked at him shrewdly before she got on to the pillion. 'Then why have you come?'

'Why shouldn't I?' he countered. 'I wanted to see you.'

Back at her lodgings she made coffee and they settled to-gether in the one big armchair by the red glow of the electric fire.

'Now you can tell me what's bothering you,' Spice said.

He told her, striving to sound indifferent, not realising that the eagerness of his expression betrayed him. She was stunned at first.

'Two years?' she echoed.

'Yes, but we could get married immediately I got back,' he told her.

She blinked quickly and he took her face between his hands, looking into her eyes.

'I won't go if you're really against it, Spice,' he promised.

She struggled up. 'It's a wonderful opportunity,' she said, 'but are you sure it's genuine?'

He told her that the agent in the port had already checked up for him that Farr was in fact the man he claimed to be.

'He's paying my passage out, anyway,' he added.

'Two years,' Spice repeated sadly.

'But . . .' he began but she cut him short.

'Oh yes, I know. We could get married immediately you come back—if you come back.' Her voice ended in a sob.

'Stop that!' he said shortly.

It was Spice's turn to take his face in her hands. 'You really are set on going, aren't you?'

David thought he would never forget her mouth shaping the question. For a moment his eyes fell. He had a fleeting treacherous memory of the 'King' once declaiming on the life of a fisherman. 'A man who has his own boat doesn't need a wife as well. He may want one, he may have one, but he doesn't need one no matter how much he thinks he does at times.'

Spice still held his face. 'Honest and truly,' she insisted. He detected the tremor in her voice and looked up to meet her eyes again.

'I don't want to leave you,' he temporised. That was true, he knew, but at the same time he acknowledged the inevitable bitterness that would assail him if he had to work as a hand on another man's boat for the next ten years knowing that if he had once had the courage to make this decision he could have been skippering his own. The words had to be said.

'Yes, I want to go, Spice. I may never have another chance like this.'

'When?' she asked.

'Next week.'

'Oh God!' she said and clung to him.

He kissed her hair and rubbed his face on hers.

'Your beard smells of fish,' she complained, and her smile was a gallant one.

'I didn't have time to shampoo it before I left,' he replied, meeting her mood.

Her eyes lingered on his face. 'You'll be all brown and handsome when you come back,' she predicted. 'Unless you let your beard grow so thick that the sun can't penetrate it.'

'I might shave it off,' he told her. 'And then when you come to meet me at the airport you'll think it's some strange man rushing up to you and trying to kiss you.'

She gave him a wise smile. 'D'you think I wouldn't recognise you with or without your beard?' she teased.

'What would you say if I did shave it off?' he questioned.

'I'd say you must put it in a bag and send it to me to fondle.'

He bit her ear. 'Spice, you'll have to promise to wait for me.' He felt he was taking a terrible risk.

'I'll wait,' she promised.

They resolved that before he left the country David should take her to meet his sister and at the same time he was to attempt to placate his parents. In the morning he was on his motor-bike again, speeding off for the port to collect his things and say his goodbyes before returning to pick up Spice and take her to his home.

The leave-taking of all his friends and of the now familiar port was sadder than he had expected it to be. He hurried over the last few minutes of saying goodbye to his landlady. As he strapped the small suitcase on his bike she stood over him solicitously until her attention was called by the postman, who handed her a letter. She held it out to David. The envelope was addressed in a thick laborious scrawl which struck him as being vaguely familiar. Opening it, he looked for the signature and saw that it was from Zannah. Thinking at first that it would be merely her good wishes for his future he started to read it through quickly, but after the first few sentences he went back and began to read again. For the second time within a few days he felt winded by the turn of events. He was aware of his landlady's troubled gaze and stuffing the letter into his pocket he bade her a final farewell and kicked the motor-cycle into action.

As soon as he reached a quiet stretch of road well away from the port he pulled in and read through the letter again.

Dear Boy, Zannah had written.

I don't get round to writing many letters so you'll excuse this if it doesn't come clear. All I ask is for the time being you don't say a word to Spice or anybody about what I have to tell you. . . .

She went on to explain that for some months she had suspected Mush was not as well as he should be and that a week ago she had at last persuaded him to see a doctor. Mush had returned saying the doctor had given him a bottle of medicine and that he would soon be all right again, but Zannah, dissatisfied, had confronted the doctor herself and had been told bluntly that Mush was in a bad way. If he did not cease heavy work immediately, the doctor said, he would be lucky if he lived another six months. The outcome of it was that Zannah had decided to retire. She was, she said, halfway through negotiations for buying a small cottage where she could look after Mush and see he took things easy.

David felt himself beginning to tremble as he read on:

It's a terrible thought to me to be leaving 'Spizannah', but there's nothing else I can do. I've had a good offer for her but the man wants her for carrying coal and I can't abide the thought of it. Not coal! Not in my old 'Spizannah'! I couldn't do that to her. So I'm thinking what would you say if I made her over to you and Spice and you could carry on the business? There's plenty of trade yet for a boat like this and I wouldn't ask you anything for her knowing that she was still part of the family and it would be less of a grief to me and Mush.

David sat on the bike, hunched against the cold wind and looking up for inspiration to a sky that was a medley of weather-shaped clouds as contrary in their predictions as was the turmoil of his own mind. What was he to do? If he acceded to Zannah's suggestion there he would be, skipper of his own boat within a month or so and without any long separation from Spice. He felt unjustifiably angry with a fate that, having given him such a battle with himself to reach one decision, had now confronted him with another of equal importance.

Leaving the bike he plodded across the moors to where a steep outcrop of stone was marked by a small cairn. He scrambled up and sat on the cairn and with the wind ushering in the first reticent snowflakes he pondered his problem.

Six months ago, even six days ago, he would have jumped at Zannah's offer, but the offer from Nelson Farr and the resolving of his own subsequent dilemma had taught him that his desire was not just for a life on the sea at any cost. Inextricably his life was bound up with fishing. He could not see himself skippering a lumbering old grandmother of a boat like the *Spizannah* while she plodded from port to port shipping and discharging cargo, but pictured himself at the helm of a lissom, high-mettled boat that could at least match the rest of the fleet in speed; he wanted the stimulation of the search, the exhilaration of filling holds; the race to harbour and the return to sea to begin again the stalking of its bounty.

The sky had turned blue with cold, the sun hung silvery and weightless as a bauble on a Christmas tree; a snow cloud rose slowly above the hills. David went back and started the bike. At the first telephone kiosk he stopped and phoned Spice, telling her that he would be delayed but without giving her any reason for it. His mind was made up and he must go to see Zannah and give her his decision.

Zannah looked only moderately surprised when she poked her head out of the hatch in answer to his hail. He thought she looked tired and wished that what he had to tell her would help to assuage her obvious grief. She sat on the bunk listening to him while her hand fondled a box of kittens, the progeny of a starving, one-eyed, half-tailed wharf cat which she had rescued and fed to butter fatness.

'A pity I didn't write a day or two earlier,' she said when he had finished. 'You might have been of a different mind then.'

He nodded a lie. *Spizannah* was a wonderful boat, he admitted it now that he was aboard her again, but he didn't want to share his boat with any woman—not even Spice. His boat must be manned by an ebullient crew, inured to the rough living of the week, content with the rough loving of the weekends. He wanted the contrasting tranquillity of a shore home, a cosy bed and a seductive wife.

'Shall you sell her?' he asked Zannah, aware of how brutal the question must sound.

'I suppose I might just as well,' she said heavily. 'Though let her go to the coal carrier I will not. I believe I'd as soon see her sink at her moorings than she should come to that.'

'Why not use her as a houseboat?' he suggested.

'I've thought of that but old Mush wouldn't take things easy enough. No, we must go and live on the land and if someone comes up with an offer for her where I won't feel she's bein' defiled I'll maybe let her go.' She patted the bunk beside her as she might have patted the neck of a favourite horse. 'Aye, but she's a good boat yet is *Spizannah*,' she said. 'But I suppose the time had to come sooner or later.'

'You'll be able to have your rose garden,' he tried to comfort her.

'Aye, thank God I've got that to look forward to. Mush'll enjoy that too.' She was quiet a moment and then she said, 'I suppose you realise I'll have to marry the old bugger now.'

David looked at her startled. 'Will you?' he asked.

'Oh, aye. Mush is funny that way. He's shared this boat with me all these years since my husband went but he says when we live on the land we must abide by land customs. He says folks will talk about us if we aren't man and wife.' She chuckled. 'Fancy that now! Me and Mush gettin' spliced. Mind you, I'm not fussy either way, but I daresay it's best to humour him.'

She pressed him to stay for a meal but he wanted to get away.

'I'd better say goodbye to Mush,' he said and stood up. Zannah got to her feet.

'Are you going to tell Spice?' he asked her.

'About me retirin' or about you refusin' the boat?' she asked, looking at him steadily. 'The way I see it is I'll have to tell her I'm retirin'.'

'Will you have to tell her about me?'

Zannah looked away. 'Not unless she asks,' she replied. 'You won't tell her yourself?'

'I'd sooner not,' he said. 'Not before I go.'

Zannah's glance was enigmatic. 'I daresay you're right,' she said.

Mush and Zannah stood on deck to watch him go. He thought, I'm glad I turned it down. Zannah's wonderful and I love every pound and every ounce of her but I wouldn't want Spice to spread as much as that.

He had written to Megan telling her they were coming and asked her to acquaint his parents with the news. As soon as the motor-cycle stopped outside Megan's home she was at the door to greet them, her face full of welcome. She was heavily pregnant and he was ashamed that he had forgotten to mention the fact to Spice. The two women went upstairs and when they returned David asked:

'Did you tell Mother and Father we were coming?'

'Yes,' Megan replied, and added meaningly, 'They're expecting you.'

He said, 'I'll go in the morning.'

It was nearing dinner-time when he walked down the

remembered street and approached the door of his parents' house. Should he knock and wait for his mother to come or should he push open the door and go straight in? His footsteps slowed unconsciously as he turned into the gate. The door of the back kitchen was partly open and he made for it. His mother was standing by the stove with her back towards him. He had an ominous feeling of repetition as he saw that she was frying fish and he again caught the smell that was so like stale lobster bait. His mother saw the vestige of his expression of distaste as she turned and her mouth tightened defensively.

'Hello, Mother!' he said, and went forward to plant a kiss on her head. She was smaller than he remembered.

'Well, boy,' she responded. Her voice was affable and he thought he detected a slight catch in it. As she put down the greasy fish-slice he saw that her hand was trembling. She turned back to the frying-pan as the fat crackled.

'Your father will be home any minute,' she told him. 'He'll be pleased to see you.'

'Good,' said David, and found he was at a loss what to say next.

Footsteps coming down the path penetrated the awkward silence. His father stood in the doorway. David held out his hand. 'Hello, Father!' he said.

'Hello, boy!' His father grasped the proffered hand but dropped it again after a perfunctory shake.

David was acutely aware of the old unhappy difference between them. His absence had not dissolved his father's antipathy, he realised, and though he was being accepted again he had not been forgiven. Cynically he attributed his acceptance to an attempt to silence the wagging tongues of neighbours and chapel folk rather than a real desire for reconciliation. He looked at his mother, wondering if in secret moments she had thought of him and wished him well, or whether her unshakable loyalty to her husband had successfully prevented her from fretting over his absence.

'Megan tells us you're going off to South Africa,' his father said as he washed his hands at the sink. David thought he caught a fleeting expression of dismay on his mother's face as she passed him, carrying the plates of food into the kitchen.

'Yes, I've been offered a good job there.'

'Still fishing?' His father's voice was edged with disapproval.

'Yes.'

'How long for?' his mother asked.

'Two years,' David told her. 'By then I hope to have enough saved to set myself up and get married.'

His father pulled noisily at the roller towel that hung behind the door. His mother's glance shot from him to David and back again.

'Have you got a girl, then?' she asked.

'I'm engaged,' David said.

His father pushed past him into the kitchen. 'I'm hungry,' he said and sat down at the table.

'You'll stay and have a bit of dinner with us?' David sensed his mother's wish for him to stay and hesitated only a moment before agreeing.

They expressed no desire to meet Spice but he took her along with him the next day to introduce her. By tacit agreement the fact that she lived on a boat was not mentioned, and when they were about to leave David's mother took him aside.

'She's not such a bad girl as I'd have expected you to choose,' she said.

His bag was packed, his ticket and passport ready. They climbed into Harry's small car for the journey to the airport where he was to meet Nelson Farr. His parents were there to see him off. His flight was called.

'Goodbye, Father,' he said, and they shook hands.

His mother was holding tight to his father's arm.

'Goodbye, Mam,' David said, not realising that he had reverted to his childhood name for her.

'Goodbye, son. Take care of yourself.' Her prim mouth twitched and for a moment her eyes had a lost look. She turned and looked up at her husband, as if reasserting her loyalty to him.

David turned to Spice. They had said their goodbyes in the privacy of Megan's home but now they clung together in a last fierce hug.

'Please choose me,' Spice whispered in his ear. Their hands slid reluctantly apart.

With Nelson Farr, David walked out to the plane, the goodbye to Spice still tearing at his insides.

'And your heart's still completely taken up with fishing?' Farr's words sounded as if they were the second half of a question already begun.

David could hear the roughness in his own voice as he answered:

'Yes, that's right. It's the fishing that I want.'

LILLIAN BECKWITH'S HEBRIDEAN TRILOGY

The Hills is Lonely

'A bouquet for Miss Beckwith ... She is a gallant woman, and she has written with brio and delight a book that will be deeply appreciated by those who value an imaginative understanding of far places.'

Eric Linklater, *John O' London's*

'After the usual pinchbeck stuff that passes for reported Highland and Hebridean speech it is a relief to read Miss Beckwith. This Englishwoman has caught the real glamour and something of the real beauty of the Western tongue.'

Moray McLaren

'A funny and enchanting book ... Miss Beckwith learned to love the life among the inhabitants of the Hebrides that she accepted with such tolerance and humour, and we are the more fortunate for her recording of it.'

Vernon Fane, *The Sphere*

Also available in Arrow Books

The Sea for Breakfast

'It would be very difficult not to enjoy *The Sea for Breakfast* . . . for the charm and simplicity of its writing, not to mention the wonderful, warm people who inhabit its covers.'

The Scotsman

'The most amusing book to come my way . . .'

The Sunday Times

The Loud Halo

'For an unsentimental, lively, apparently photographically accurate picture of life on a Hebridean island, Miss Beckwith's essays or memoirs or stories would be hard to beat.'

The Times

If you would like a complete list of Arrow books please send a postcard to Arrow Books Ltd, 178-202 Great Portland Street, London W1